M. AINIHI

Lost

A Blood Inheritance Novel

First edition

Editing by Allister Thompson
Illustration by Tauseef Ahmed
Cover art by rebecacover

This book was professionally typeset on Reedsy.
Find out more at reedsy.com

*This book is gratefully dedicated
to Frank*

Contents

Acknowledgement iii

Amanda - Monsters and Memories 1

Emily - The Escape 11

Emily - Carpool 24

Amanda - Tempers, Riddles, and Myths 31

Emily - Dumpster Diving 44

Emily - Town Limits 54

Amanda - Hard Release 60

Kiami - Siren Song 72

Kiami - The Owl and The Unicorn 78

Amanda - Excitement and Jealousy 85

Amanda - Jinn and Spies 91

Kiami - Black Diamond 97

Emily - Weeds 104

Emily - Collision Course 119

Emily - Expulsion 130

Amanda - Strange Premonitions 140

Emily - The Cost of Magic 143

Emily - Fierce, Fiery Friends 151

Kiami - Advantages for Owls 160

Kiami - Eyewitness 168

Amanda - Dreams and Schemes 173

Kiami - Defector 176

Kiami – Snooping   181
Emily – Belonging   185
Emily – The Barefoot Spy's Tale   197
Amanda – A New Host   203
Emily – Second Thoughts   207
Kiami – We Are All Monsters   210
Emily – The Jinn's Request   218
Emily – On Shaky Ground   228
Amanda – Brewing Storm   235
Best-Laid Plans...   241
Oh, Rats!   252
Catching On   267
About the Author   271
Also by M. Ainihi   272

Acknowledgement

I want to thank my husband, and the rest of my family, who continue to support and encourage my publishing endeavors.

To all the freelancers I have had the opportunity to work with on The Blood Inheritance Novels, including but not limited to, artists, illustrators, graphic designers, cover designers, various editors, and logo designers you have my deepest gratitude. It is an honor to work with so many talented individuals from all over the globe.

1

Amanda - Monsters and Memories

Amanda worked shrouded in the darkness of the castle library. Only the dim glow of a single candle flame penetrated the room as she wrote in frantic bursts, letting her thoughts spill over the paper.

She had pushed open the carefully constructed wall that barricaded her from the memories of the time before she had been brought to the Arcane realm by the sorcerer Jacob and let them run loose in her head as she scribbled.

She hoped it would help to erase from her mind the image of the terrible creature that invaded her sleep. She could still smell the foul odor of his breath as if he hovered over her now, staring at her with bloodshot eyes.

A tangled mass of forest-green hair puffed up from the top of his head, making the dull gray sheen of his skin more pronounced, and when he lifted the corners of his mouth into a wide smile, pointed yellow teeth protruded from the edges of his thin lips.

As disturbing as she found his appearance, for the first few months she had no trouble returning to sleep after these encounters, but then the whispers began. As he leaned in, his hunched back protruded through a hole in his worn-out shirt, and she swore she could feel his hot breath against her face as he spoke. Her name sounded like nails against a blackboard in his gravelly voice.

The troubling nightmares had begun shortly after she and Aden had freed themselves from Jacob, and even as the frequency increased over time, she hadn't thought much about them. In fact, after everything she had encountered, having a few nightmares seemed pretty normal.

The more he spoke in the coming weeks, the harder she attempted to shut him out, believing the creature to be a figment of her own creation caused by the repression of her memories.

Is it all in my head?

She looked down at the large purple welt that circled her arm and wondered if she could have managed to inflict the bruise on herself as she slept fitfully, causing the image of the monster to squeeze her arm in her dream state.

Long ago, her father had suggested to her that writing was a good way to get something off your chest, especially if that something should remain unspoken, and it seemed to be working. With each new sentence, she felt the knot that had formed in the pit of her stomach loosen.

She traced the outline of the bruise with tip of her index finger. Either way, she needed to find relief from the dreams.

Whether or not the monster was in her head, he seemed to want her to remember all the things she had buried deep in her mind, and she hoped at the very least the exercise would satisfy the creature into allowing her a few nights' sleep.

Before she had uncovered the artifact in the woods and learned that the Human realm was just one of many, she had been an average teenage girl, or at least that's what she had been raised to believe.

Amanda wondered if anything would have turned out differently if she hadn't released the jinni, Erol, from the artifact that served as his prison. She had been connected to the jinni when she summoned him — a connection that wouldn't have allowed her to keep her secrets locked away so easily.

She paused her writing to look up at the candle flame, concentrating on making it glow brighter. She didn't share that connection with Aden. She felt a wet tear roll down her cheek and brushed it away. *Aden would never understand; he had no choice but to obey the sorcerer during his imprisonment.*

In a way, she envied him for that, because the choices she had been given after her capture had all seemed wrong. Aden had been kidnapped by the sorcerer when he was still a young jinni.

Amanda was curious if the two artifacts were somehow connected. The enchanted knife the sorcerer had used to enslave him had held similar runic symbols to Erol's prison, even though his had been created by arcane magic instead of the magic of the jinn.

3

Although she no longer had Erol's prison, the image of her standing in her kitchen, scrubbing the dirt loose from its carvings was fresh in her mind. She reached up to touch the scars that Jacob had cut into her shoulders; some of the images were identical to the runes present on the two relics.

Wondering at the significance of the symbols on the artifacts, Amanda turned the paper sideways and wrote *RUNES?* along the edge. She knew her scars represented the realms; Jacob had carved them there to allow her easier travel between them.

Despite the spell he had cast over her that allowed her to read the secret language of the Arcane sorcerer, she realized she didn't know what each individual symbol meant. Amanda furrowed her brow. *Maybe this is what I need to remember?*

Amanda shrugged and turned the page back around to read over the first sentence she had jotted: **Am I a hero or a villain?**

Even if the sorcerer hadn't lied about wanting the ring to control the jinn, I would still feel like a villain. In truth, he had sensed the dormant power within her and had used her as his pawn while he worked to bring it to the surface. *I did almost everything that he wanted me to; I was his puppet.*

The hair bristled on the back of her neck as she continued to skim what she had written.

I was just a girl trying to do the right thing ... at least that's how I recall it, but as the days go by, I can't help but ask. This question has been gnawing at me for some time, and as the search for my mother continues to come up empty, the hole in my heart continues to grow, not because we haven't found her, but because I am not sure I want to. The truth is I am afraid of what I will find if I meet her.

Could my father have been keeping other secrets from me? Amanda rolled her eyes. *Stop feeling sorry for yourself.* She had no real proof that he had known about the realms or that her mother was not human, and wondering would do her no good. She would never have the chance to ask him.

If the jinn could grant wishes, as they did in human myth, I would turn back time. But they can't, and nothing I do will bring back the things I have lost.

I want to forget about the choices I have had to make since I first encountered Erol's artifact in the woods, and the things the sorcerer stole from me when he dragged me into his fiendish plot. I only knew that if his evil was allowed to grow, he would not only destroy us, but also everything that is wonderful about the world.

Is it really better to sacrifice the few to save the many, and in making that choice did I condemn myself to a lifetime of darkness?

Out of necessity, I attempted to embrace the shadow magic that I inherited from my mother, but it is stronger than me, and I can feel it growing day by day with every move I make. I fear it will take over by the time I am through.

Amanda sucked in her breath. *If the Human realm was created only for humans, then where could I ever fit in?* The realms were separated by some type of veil-like barricade meant to keep the magical races from interacting with humans. She let the air out of her lungs. *I don't belong anywhere. This is as close to home as I will ever come.* She forced her eyes back to the page.

I searched these books trying to find a way to save us all from Jacob, and for that, Aden says I am a hero, even if lives were lost. He claims that he is proud to stand with me, telling me not to regret and not to fear. But that's easy for him to say; he doesn't have a monster visiting his dreams, spreading seeds of doubt.

At first I thought the vile creature was a figment of my imagination, guilt spilling over into my dreams, but now I am not so sure. He has stopped whispering about the past and has begun telling me about my future...

So I need to tell myself something before it's too late.

The flame bent backward as the door to the library opened. Amanda folded the paper and slid it into a book at random before moving it on top of one of the piles in front of her.

She allowed a smile to spread across her lips. "Hello, Aden."

She pushed the heavy wooden chair back and stood to face him. "Are you ready to go back to the tomb?" Aden asked halfheartedly. "We don't have to. We can try to talk to Bloise again."

She crossed her arms over her chest and cocked an eyebrow. "That old wizard made it clear that he will only help if he thinks he's getting something out of it. Besides, I have a hunch that the pretty little jinni will be there this time."

"Do you think she will remember the day that you and Erol visited? It seems like it was so long ago."

Amanda hesitated, recalling the jinni's unusual yellow eyes and wondering if it were possible she could have dismissed Amanda from her own thoughts after that day. She searched her memory, trying to recall how much of the encounter she had told Aden.

Aden's green eyes seemed to bore holes into her as he waited for her to respond. "I think it was a pretty memorable experience." Amanda dropped her arms and moved to stand beside the desk. "Did you know that the tomb is said to attract lost items and hidden knowledge?" She reached forward and picked up a book, only to place it right back down on another pile.

"You have mentioned it before, yes."

Amanda cocked her head, remembering how the walls had threatened to cave in on them with the combined magic of her mother's ancestry and the black diamond Erol had given her before her life spun out of control...

The day they arrived at the tomb had been the first time her shadow magic showed itself. The wave of unfamiliar power had pushed at her, begging to be released, and in her anger she had. *Why?*

She reached down and traced her fingers over the bulge of the gem in her pocket. She had lost the gift when Jacob had kidnapped her and brought her to the Arcane realm, but it had been returned

7

to her that day ... right before the spider landed on her, pushing her over the edge. She had been upset with Erol, and the magic that was welling up inside of her had burst out.

The memory stung. She sucked in a deep breath and exhaled slowly as she moved around a few more books at random. "Her name is *Jacqueline*, and I will bring the gem in case she has forgotten me. She is the one that insisted I kept it, after all, and even if she knows nothing of my mother, she must know something about the black diamond."

Amanda looked back over her shoulder at him as he pushed his dark hair away from his forehead. His lips were pressed into a straight line.

"What's wrong now?" she groaned as she turned the rest of her body around to face him.

"Nothing, it's just ... I don't remember you calling the jinni by name before." He took a step toward her and reached out to place a hand on her arm. "If there's something you're not telling me..." He cleared his throat and looked up to meet her eyes before starting again. "You do know you can tell me anything, Amanda."

She clenched her fist at her side and bit her tongue. *I wish that were true.*

Like the monster that invaded her sleep, she kept her visions to herself. They were her burdens to bear, especially now, if the monster was in fact not all in her head. He had to be connected to the visions and therefore somehow connected to Jacqueline.

Amanda thought about her most recent experience. It hadn't been the first time she was thrust behind this particular young woman's eyes, but it was the first time she had ever seen a familiar face during a vision. When the jinni had appeared, the girl had called her name and pleaded to her for help. Instead, Jacqueline had fled.

Frustrated, Amanda wrinkled her nose, trying to recall the reason she had been so sure that the jinni was heading back to the tomb, but the finer details of the vision were already fading from her memory. She needed to find a way to get a real night's sleep soon.

"It just seems like a fitting name, that's all." Amanda choked out the lie, reminding herself he was safer not knowing about the nightmares or the visions.

She relaxed her fist and gave his hand a reassuring pat before turning back to the desk once again, eying the heaped-up books.

No longer sure which one she had placed her note inside, she sighed and bent down to blow out the candle. She had a better chance of finding the letter in the tomb than ever coming across it again amidst the mess in front of her.

None of this is Aden's fault. She spun back around to face him with a fresh smile. "I guess I am ready if you are." She winked and grabbed hold of his arm. "Just keep a watchful eye out for spiders when we get inside."

Amanda knew that time moved much faster in the Human realm, and she had no way of knowing how much had passed since she had her last vision. If they didn't hurry, they could miss

Jacqueline altogether.

As she wrapped her arm around his waist, he winced but didn't say anything. Amanda glanced at the dull gray bracelets she had slid onto her arm, wondering if they could be made of iron or perhaps if they had a spell cast upon them. She had found them in with Jacob's things, after all. But before she could question Aden, the scene around her shifted and fell away as he guided her out of the Arcane realm to look for Jacqueline.

2

Emily - The Escape

Emily pressed the payphone to her ear and listened to the tone. She dialed quickly before she could lose her nerve. Her hand trembled as she held the receiver. She just needed to hear Vanessa's voice.

"Hello?"

Tears of relief filled Emily's eyes. *She is safe.*

"Hello?" Vanessa repeated. "Em?" She was whispering now.

Emily's pulse skipped, hearing her name.

"Em, it's okay." Concern had crept into the voice. "Where are you?

Emily remained silent; she was afraid to respond, scared of what her friend might ask. She dropped the phone onto the cradle and crumpled onto the sidewalk. Her eyes welled with tears. If anyone noticed her sitting there in her state, they gave no indication as they hurried past.

Emily tried to get her thoughts together. The scene had been replaying through her mind over and over all night, and she was exhausted.

Not thinking, she had acted on impulse.

Emily watched as her best friend walked out onto the diving board, waving to her. Emily smiled up from her lounge chair and waved back. Her eyes were trained on Vanessa as she took three quick steps to the end, one foot slipping as she leapt up and out.

Emily had seen the outcome almost before it happened. She was already leaping into the water as she heard the sick thud sound of Vanessa's head hitting the edge of the diving board.

Her eyes stung as she searched for her friend's body at the bottom of the pool. She could hear the muffled sounds of whistles and people shouting from above. She could see the blood swirling, dancing around the girl's hair. As Emily pulled her up to the surface, Vanessa's body felt limp in her arms.

Emily cupped Vanessa's mouth and nose with her hand and felt no breath coming from her lips. Someone was calling frantically for her to bring Vanessa to the edge of the pool. She heard a splash as someone else jumped in and hurried toward the pair.

Emily felt it suddenly: the sound of static filled her ears. The pressure built quickly from somewhere deep inside. She didn't bother to try to hold it in; she could think of nothing but the girl in her arms as she allowed the growing energy to release from her in a fast, crashing wave.

Someone was tugging at them, trying to remove them from the pool. Her friend gasped, and water spilled from her mouth. Emily let out a relieved breath. The pounding in her chest slowed, and she loosened her grip on Vanessa. The lifeguard managed to pull the girl from Emily's arms as she stood shoulder-deep in the pool, stunned by what had just played out.

Fresh panic set in as Emily realized what she had done. The thing she was never supposed to do, a thing she had only done once before, and it had changed everything.

Emily took a deep breath trying to appear calm as she pulled herself from the pool, her heart racing again. She could already hear the ambulance siren in the distance. She would only have a few minutes to get out of there.

As she snatched up her backpack and headed toward the door, one of the lifeguards grabbed her arm, startling her. "Not a scratch on..."

Emily ripped herself loose before he could finish his sentence, leaving him in stunned silence. She had no doubt that they would find blood on the diving board, and when they did, they would have questions she couldn't answer.

She ran then, still barefoot, out the exit and across the hot pavement. Emily didn't dare to stop until she was gasping for breath. Shaking from the overexertion, she fumbled with the zipper on her backpack and pulled her dry clothing on over her damp bathing suit. She gave up trying to tie her shoelaces and tucked them into the sides of her sneakers. She reached her arm out and steadied herself against a tree as a wave of nausea overtook her.

Once her stomach settled, she glanced around the park to get her bearings. She shivered even as the afternoon sun beat down on her.

A few curious parents watched her with obvious concern at her strange, erratic behavior. One woman stared at Emily so intently that she failed to notice her son beside her, filling his mouth with blades of freshly plucked grass. Emily forced a smile at them as she shouldered her backpack and walked toward the highway and away from the suburb where she had grown up.

Emily knew hitchhiking was dangerous, especially for a young teen on her own. She thought of the cul-de-sac where she lived with her parents, a loop of identical houses with white picket fences. *No.* She shook her head. That place hadn't been home for a long time. Home was supposed to be a refuge; hers was more like a prison.

She had once felt comforted by the light pink color of her small bedroom. The decals of castles that still plastered the walls were now inappropriate for a fifteen-year-old. The only addition since her eleventh birthday was the lock that had been installed on the outside of her bedroom door: the punishment for the one time she had shown them her gift, or her curse. Emily wasn't sure what it was anymore.

The thing she hated most about the room wasn't the childish

décor or the fact that she was locked in there nightly, but rather the word "princess" that had been so carefully painted above her twin bed by her once loving and adoring parents. The word served as a reminder of all that she had lost on that birthday.

Emily walked along the shoulder of the highway, thumb out. She would take her chances. She wasn't sure where she would go or what she would find. She knew only one thing for certain: whatever the danger was on the road, it would pale in comparison to what she would find if she returned to her parents.

Emily stood and wiped her face with her sleeve. She suddenly felt very small amidst the towering buildings around her. She needed to find a cheap place to stay for the night, one where they wouldn't ask too many questions.

She turned away from the bustling streets where people in crisp suits and heels hurried with cell phones pressed against their ears. Away from the extravagant buildings that were fitted so closely together; you couldn't have squeezed a penny in between them.

She walked toward the less crowded streets and on until she was in an area where the buildings were spread farther apart, but just far enough to leave dark alleyways. These alleyways were home to dumpsters and scattered crates. Some had people sleeping in them, covered only by a thin sheet of cardboard. One had two men fist-fighting over something, and Emily hurried past, trying not to look at the men as they threw punches and words. The buildings here seemed older, almost decaying, and they loomed menacingly above her.

Finally, she saw a half-lit sign in the distance and picked up her pace. As she drew closer to the motel, she could hear the hum of fluorescent bulbs. The building was in need of new paint, and the steps creaked each time she placed a foot down. She took a deep breath and walked inside. The front office smelled musty, and Emily crinkled her nose.

An open pizza box rested on the countertop, half full, and she had to stop herself from grabbing a slice. Her stomach rumbled. She couldn't remember the last time she had eaten. A round bell sat next to the register, and Emily slapped her hand down on it, still eyeing the pizza box.

She wasn't quite prepared for the sudden appearance of the round, balding man. Her smile faltered momentarily as she took in his stained white shirt and grungy ripped shorts.

"What do you want?" he grumbled as he grabbed a slice of pizza from the box and proceeded to stuff half of it into his mouth.

Emily cleared her throat and tried to stand a little taller. "A room, please." Her voice faltered at the end, so it came out more like a question than a statement.

The man wiped his hands on his shirt and pulled a clipboard from somewhere under the counter. "Sixty dollars per night."

"The sign says forty," Emily said.

"Yeah, and I don't suppose your mom's outside waiting for you, is she?" he said flatly. "How old are you?"

"Eighteen," Emily blurted. She had practiced the lie over and over in her head while she walked.

"Yeah, how about that? Me too," he said. "Listen, it's sixty dollars a night. Put a name down on the paper and you get a key."

Emily reluctantly handed half of her cash over to him and signed the page.

He glanced at the clipboard and scooped up the money. "Well, Jamie Smith, I hope you enjoy your stay here." He handed over the key and winked at her. "You can call me John. John Doe, And Jamie, if you need anything, do hesitate to ask." She could still hear him laughing as she made her way out the door and along the side of the building.

Emily turned the key over in her hand and looked for the door with the matching number. Inside, she locked it behind her before she even bothered to find the light switch. There was not much to investigate in the small, cream-colored room. The green and yellow bedspread hurt her eyes. She pulled the matching curtains closed and set her backpack down in the wooden chair beside the window.

A tear slid down her cheek. Emily brushed it off and sucked in a deep breath. She had known this day would come sooner or later.

She couldn't have allowed Vanessa to die any more than she could have left that poor broken bird on her lawn four years ago, not after she felt the power inside her. Even though she had not used it since that day, she still remembered the sudden knowledge that she could change things, the realization that she could help. It had been like a switch was flipped on as soon as she had seen the helpless creature wounded on the ground.

Emily wondered if it had always been inside of her, dormant, waiting for a chance to show itself. Was it a gift? A natural talent she was born with? Or was it a curse, as her mother had called it? A punishment for something ... but what could she be punished for? She had only been a child.

Either way, it didn't matter; she wouldn't be given a third chance.

The bathroom was lacking a large towel. Emily considered using the old rotary phone to request one, but decided she would rather not see Mr. John Doe again anytime soon. She showered and did her best to dry her mass of wet hair with the hand towel that had been provided.

She combed her fingers through it and stared at her reflection in the mirror. Nothing had changed about her in the last twenty-four hours, and yet everything had changed. Again. Emily yanked on one of the purple strands that weaved its way among her jet-black curls. She winced at the pain and rubbed her scalp. She had never understood the changes that had happened to her over the last four years.

Emily's stomach growled loudly, and she thought of the pizza box.

Before everything had changed, she and her mother had on occasion accompanied her father on his business trips. She searched the room for the customary local phone book that had always been present.

Emily dropped to her knees and peered under the bed, scanning the items that had been swept beneath it. A smile spread across her face as her eyes landed on a single red sock. The sock was draped over a small yellow book. She pushed the mounting dust bunnies out of her way and retrieved her prize. She flipped slowly through the pages, considering her options. Her supply of cash was dwindling fast.

She chose the cheapest pizza chain she could find. Vanessa had always referred to it as cardboard pizza, and she usually agreed — not that she had many hot meals at her house. At least not since her parents stopped inviting her to join them for dinner.

She had become accustomed to eating alone and preparing meals by herself. She would eat dinner before her parents came home from work. The refrigerator and cupboards were always stocked, so she knew they didn't want her to starve. They just wanted to pretend she didn't exist. Her bedroom door was always unlocked again in the morning, right before they left the house.

Emily jumped at the knock on the door. She had only a vague recollection of making the call. She pulled the side of the curtain away from the window and peeked out at the gangly boy clothed in sagging jeans and a t-shirt. He clutched the strap to the insulated red delivery bag in one hand. The other remained frozen, hovering in front of the door, poised to knock again.

Emily stepped back from the window, releasing the curtain and calling out, "One sec," as she rummaged for a twenty-dollar bill.

She unlocked the door and pulled it open, reaching toward the boy with the cash. "Keep the change."

He smirked at her. "Gee, thanks."

The seconds it took for him to reach around for his wallet and deposit the cash felt like minutes. As he opened the insulated bag, the aroma of the pizza caused her stomach to release another large growl.

The delivery boy cocked an eyebrow. "Hungry?" He winked at her before extending the box in her direction.

Emily felt her face heat up, and she grabbed at the pizza, yanking it from his outstretched hand. The delivery boy took a step back as Emily spun around and slammed the door.

She returned to the window and peered back out. The pizza boy moved farther from her door then turned back, calling to her, "You have a nice night." He reached up and scratched the back of his head before moving away into the dark parking lot and out of Emily's view.

She ate the pizza greedily and lay down on top of the bed cover, feeling exhausted. An uncomfortable tightness had been present in her chest since she had run from the pool, and it still lingered.

Emily woke feeling uneasy. The room was still dark, except for a faint outline of light peeking in around the curtain. She sat up slowly, unable to shake the feeling that someone was watching her. She held her breath and strained her ears, trying to hear. Her skin was crawling; something was not right. Deciding the bathroom was her best option, she jumped from the bed and into the small room, locking the door behind her.

She pressed her back against the thin wooden door and listened for any movement. It felt like minutes had passed, and still Emily heard nothing. She shook her head in disbelief. *Could I be any more paranoid?*

A movement in the mirror caught her eye, and she smiled at the small blue reflection in the glass. The wispy ball of smoke circled her, and she giggled with uneasy relief. She reached toward the thing, and her hand passed straight through.

"Why are you here?" Emily asked, knowing she wouldn't get an answer. She glanced around, expecting to find another one hovering nearby.

The wisps had first appeared to her the night the lock had been installed on the outside of her bedroom door. Emily hadn't seen them again until a year later, on the night she had missed curfew. Until that night, she had held out hope that things could one day return to normal.

Barely twelve at the time, Emily had almost left then, but the wisps had appeared, and comforted by their strange glow, she found herself able to fall asleep curled up on the picnic table. She had tried to research the wisps at school but had never been able to find what she considered the right match.

The wisp started to dart around the bathroom, as if frantically looking for an escape.

"Fine then," Emily said out loud as she turned to the door and pulled it open. A figure stood there directly in front of her, breathing heavily. The man had on the same clothing as the night before, and Emily was surrounded by his pungent odor as he grinned at her.

"John Doe?" she squeaked.

"Who were you talking to?" he asked. Emily tried to respond, to demand the intruder get out, but she couldn't seem to find her voice again. She took a step back from him, and he quickly took one forward, trapping her inside the small bathroom, making his ghoulish intent obvious.

What is wrong with him? she wondered as he grabbed her arm, pushing her against the wall. Beads of sweat trickled down his forehead as he furrowed his brows in anger. She knew he wanted to hurt her. She could see it in his eyes. Something had changed in them; they never seemed to stop moving as they darted wildly about in his head.

Emily knew that he thought she didn't stand a chance. His nails seemed unusually sharp as they bit into the flesh of her arm. She tried to pull away from his painful grip, but he was too strong.

John bared his yellow, pointed teeth like a dog and lunged, as if trying to bite her. *Were they pointed before?* Emily squeezed her eyes shut, expecting contact.

His jaw snapped closed with such sudden force that Emily could hear the teeth knock together.

Desperately struggling, she barely had time to register the static sound in her head as a wave of pressure expelled outward, pushing him back to release his hold.

"I had no choice," she said out loud as the man in front of her stood suddenly clutching his chest. *Or control,* she thought. His mouth gaped open as he gasped for breath, revealing two rows of grimy, flat teeth. His eyes no longer moved frantically as they grew wide and he collapsed to his knees. She reached forward and grabbed his hand, examining the red, crusty residue that outlined his short nails. *Pizza sauce?*

Confused, Emily dropped his hand and shook her head, whispering to herself this time. "I know what I saw. He was ... inhuman." She scurried around him just as he began to tilt forward, falling onto his face. Emily couldn't bring herself to bend down to check his pulse. She didn't want to be that close to him ever again.

"I had no choice," she whispered, reaching for her backpack. She would walk out the door and never look back. Instead, she knelt on the floor, clutching the canvas to her chest. She hadn't wanted to hurt anyone, not even in self-defense. Maybe her parents had been right all along. *I am cursed.*

Heading toward the city had been a mistake. One she vowed never to make again. As she stood and shouldered her bag, she turned the handle and stepped outside. She locked the door before closing it behind her.

3

Emily - Carpool

Emily didn't think twice about the idling car in the parking lot as she passed it. She had only been walking for a few minutes and was trying to keep her mind from returning to what was a few blocks behind her.

She wouldn't have noticed it at all if the woman hadn't called to her, beckoning her to the passenger-side window. Turning hesitantly toward the sound, she wondered if the woman had mistaken her for someone else.

"Hi there. You look lost. Is everything okay?" The woman sounded concerned.

Emily nodded and bit her lower lip as she studied the white car and its driver. *Was this woman waiting for someone?*

"Come closer, I won't bite."

That's what they all say, Emily thought as she took a few steps toward the vehicle. The woman's light brown hair was twisted haphazardly into a bun on the top of her head. A few loose strands dangled by her glasses as they tilted on the end of her sharp nose. She had pushed them out of the way several times while signaling Emily to come closer. With each attempt, the loose strands fell right back into her face.

She looks like a school librarian, Emily thought. She was temporarily transfixed as she caught the gaze of the woman's icy blue eyes.

"I'm just on my way home." As she walked the last few steps toward the car, she noticed that the back seat was littered with black and white worksheets containing images that were mostly colored outside of the lines. Red letter grades and check marks could be seen on several of the pages. *A teacher?* she wondered, now curious. A smooth black case lay open on the back seat. It reminded her of the one she would see her mom carry down the driveway on her way to work.

Emily felt new relief with the knowledge that she would no longer have to wait and watch out her small bedroom window as her parents walked down the driveway, her mother's heels clicking with each step, smiling and waving to the neighbors as if everything was normal. Her mother's makeup would be smoothed on perfectly and evenly. Her father, when he wasn't away on a business trip, following close behind, dressed in a flawless suit and tie, would always reach up and straighten it at the knot right before he opened the car door for her mother.

The woman cleared her throat and pointed at Emily. "You're bleeding."

Emily realized she was still staring at the woman and quickly averted her eyes to where she had felt the man's claws tear at her flesh. She couldn't keep the monstrous image of John Doe from resurfacing in her mind. *But he didn't have claws or pointed teeth.* She bit her lip harder, trying to come up with some way to explain the ripped sleeve and the blood that oozed from her flesh. *Am I going crazy?* She felt her face get warm with embarrassment at her continued silence, and she turned away ready to leave but paused as the woman spoke again.

"Wait ... I have some bandages in my first aid kit." The woman fidgeted with her necklace.

Emily shook her head. "No, thank you." She couldn't help but notice the shining kaleidoscope of colors the stone on the chain contained, nothing like the amethyst she kept with her at all times. The one she had gotten for her eleventh birthday. Emily tried to remember the name — *opal?* She thought back to when she had looked into her own gem.

"Can I drop you off somewhere? I'm headed out of the city myself."

I must look really naive, Emily thought. She shuffled her feet and shifted her backpack, trying to decide how to respond. *No, I look scared and lost and hurt.* The woman must have sensed her reluctance.

"Banana?" she offered.

Banana? Emily couldn't help but look as a yellow object suddenly appeared in the woman's outstretched hand. Emily opened her mouth to refuse but instead found herself reaching for it. *I'm not even hungry.*

"Thank you," Emily responded automatically as she peeled the banana.

"I have more around here somewhere," the woman said as she turned in her seat and plucked another from somewhere in the back of the vehicle. "I'm Bav." Once again she reached toward the open window. Her eyes were light and inviting, and her smile stretched from ear to ear.

"No, thank you," Emily replied but returned Bav's smile "It's nice to meet you." *She seems nice enough. If I can sit still long enough, maybe I can come up with a plan.* She glanced at her sleeve, now caked with blood. *I do need to do something about that.*

Bav reached for the stone on her necklace again. She held it between her two fingers and rubbed it lightly. "Well, come on, get in. I do have a schedule to keep."

Emily reached for the handle, as if on automatic pilot. "Thanks." She sat in the leather-covered seat, her backpack stowed on the floor by her feet. She had one fleeting thought as the car pulled away with her in it: *Never take rides from strangers.*

Emily patched up her arm with the contents of Bav's first-aid kit as they left the city in the distance. Once the wounds were covered, she worked at the sleeve with a moist towelette, trying to remove the stains. *That will have to be good enough,* she thought, giving up on the now copper-colored smudges.

"So are you a teacher?" Emily asked to break the silence.

"Well, yes ... sort of, I definitely teach people things... How did you ... oh." She glanced at the backseat, her toothy grin widening.

"What do you teach?" Emily asked.

Bav held the stone that hung from her neck, ignoring the question. "So how old are you?" she asked, letting go of the opal.

Emily tried to sound confident in her response. "I'm eighteen. It's a curse, really, the fact that I look so young." She couldn't help but notice Bav's grin falter.

"Why are you alone, anyway?" A thin smile forced its way back onto Bav's face as she awaited Emily's reply.

Emily turned away to look out her window. She didn't want to see Bav's face as she lied to her again. Bav had already helped her so much. "I was away for school, and my mother became ill. I didn't have the money for a ticket, so I'm trying to get to her as fast as I can." Emily did her best to make the fast lie as believable as possible.

She squinted, trying to make out the shapes in the fields as they passed. She kept catching an odd trail of blue light it the distance. *How fast do we have to be going to make a light trail like that?*

Emily felt the car accelerate and turned back to Bav. She tried to catch a glimpse of the speedometer and couldn't help but notice that Bav had very large and rather hairy feet for a woman with such a delicate frame. *Who drives barefoot?* Afraid she was going to start laughing, she turned back to the passenger-side window. She felt guilty for wanting to laugh and hoped that she could keep a straight face.

Emily noticed even more of the blue streaks. They almost appeared to be trying to keep up with the car. *What in the world could they be?* Emily stared hard out the window. The blue trails reminded her of the wisp in the bathroom. She picked up her backpack and opened the small pocket in the front. Holding her amethyst always helped her feel calmer.

"Ah, you should come to my house for dinner!" Bav exclaimed with such sudden excitement that Emily jumped in her seat, momentarily forgetting what she was looking for.

Dinner? Emily thought, shivering as a picture of herself getting tossed into a large oven as Bav cackled endlessly popped into her head.

"I—I, need to get out. I ... I'm feeling sick." With her backpack clutched to her chest, Emily pulled at the handle, but the door was locked. *Good thing, too*, she thought as she pictured herself rolling out of the moving vehicle along the gravel.

"We can't stop now; we have only just begun," the lady said sternly.

Emily turned back to Bav. Her eyes didn't seem to be focused on Emily or the road as they darted wildly about in her head. Emily's stomach turned. She was now sure of what the blue streaks were trailing behind them; it was a warning.

"Em, come on, we can be good friends." Bav's voice was almost a growl at the end.

Emily reached into her backpack for the amethyst, hoping it would give her courage, and clutched it. "Stop!" she screamed at the top of her lungs. "Just stop. I need to get out, now."

The tires squealed as Bav brought the car to a sudden stop, forcing Emily's body forward painfully.

"Well, why didn't you just say so?" Bav shot her an uneasy grin, and her eyes now focused on Emily's hand. "I just got a bit excited. I haven't been to this realm in ages," she muttered.

Realm? This woman is insane, Emily pulled the lock up and jumped from the car, ready to run. Just as she decided on a direction, Bav peeled out, leaving a trail of dust and Emily behind.

Emily shook her head in disbelief. She had heard the world referred to as a crazy place, but this was unbelievable. *Maybe I'm a magnet for bad things.*

She stared straight ahead, detesting the sight of the road. It rolled on and on into the distance and never seemed to end. She waited, standing still for a few minutes, expecting the wisps to show up. *Was it my imagination? Were they ever really there?*

She thought about running into the field if she heard a car. It was thick with tall corn stalks and seemed like a good place to hide. *Or to get lost.*

Emily knew she needed a plan. But an urgency to move forward tugged at her. She walked on, continuing in the direction she had been traveling with Bav.

4

Amanda - Tempers, Riddles, and Myths

Amanda rested her head on her hand and yawned. She had been tired before she traveled with Aden to the tomb; now she was wrung out and exhausted. The grinning monster continued to haunt her dreams, taunting her, asking questions she refused to hear, and since she had brought Jacqueline back from the tomb the with her, his efforts had seemed to double. She rarely slept at all.

"I really have no idea what I am doing," she whispered to herself. "If I did, I wouldn't have fallen for Jacqueline's tricks in the first place." The strange responses she got from Jacqueline only gave her more questions to add to the ones she had. *They can see, and their roots grow so deep. They have eyes everywhere.' What does that even mean?* "Nonsense, gibberish, that's what."

It had been a combination of temper and luck that put her in this situation to begin with. *Was it really luck?* If she were to believe the monster, she had planned to kidnap Jacqueline from the beginning.

She looked up into the round mirror attached to the table in front of her. The skin below her eyes looked dark and puffy. Behind her, the reflection of her unmade bed called her to return, even as the monster's words echoed in her head.

'You can't keep ignoring me, Amanda. You cannot hide from the darkness within you.' His face had loomed over her, blocking the view beyond him. This time, when she had tried to turn her face, she found she couldn't look away from his inhuman grin.

Not wanting to risk falling back asleep, Amanda lifted her head and straightened her back against her seat; she'd had enough of her nightmare monster for one evening

Her eyes shifted to the black diamond that lay on the table in front of her. She couldn't help but wonder whether or not she would have been as quick to lose her temper at the tomb with Jacqueline, if she hadn't had it in her pocket, and the bracelets... "Maybe the monster is right," she breathed.

Even before she had been brought to the Arcane realm, she had only worn jewelry on a rare occasion, so why had she slid the uninteresting metal rings onto her arm when she found them? Had she hoped deep down, even before Aden had shied away from them, that the dull gray metal held some sort of power?

Once secured on Jacqueline's wrists, the bracelets seemed to dampen the jinni's magic just enough to stop her from retaliating. *If he was right about that, maybe he was right about other things.*

Amanda had seen iron used to stop jinn from utilizing their gifts in the past, and with that knowledge she deduced that the bracelets, although not pure iron, had to at least contain trace amounts of the metal.

She pushed herself up from the chair and shook her head. She had merely reacted to the jinni's strange behavior to the best of her ability.

What provoked the jinni to begin with? Maybe she was just on alert because she wasn't able to make herself unseen to me. Amanda began to pace the small room. *No, she was up to something before*

we arrived at the tomb, and our appearance startled her.

Even without the extra power from the diamond in her pocket, dark, shadowy places often made the magic within her more pronounced. Startled, Aden had gripped Amanda's arm so tightly that she had pushed the wave of magic from within her out at Jacqueline, even before he had managed to yank her backward.

The jinni had been chanting while clearing her items from the floor in a rush. *What was she doing, casting some sort of silencing spell?*

"It doesn't make any sense." *Why would she do that unless she knew more than she was telling? I should have been better prepared for something like that. After all, jinn are mischievous.* She scowled and slid back into the chair, laying her head down on her arm. *This jinni in particular seems more artful in her responses by the day.*

But there was something else that had gleamed in her eyes beyond recognition of Amanda and what she had become. *Fear?* Amanda lifted her head and tapped her nails on the desk. *She sure doesn't seem afraid now that she is a prisoner. Could she have known that I saw her by the sea?* Goosebumps formed on her arms as she recalled what had happened during the vision, right before Jacqueline had shown up, but trying to recall the sharp details of the event was useless. *Maybe it isn't me that she's afraid of. Maybe she knows of my nightmare monster...*

She shifted in the uncomfortable chair as she reviewed her options. She knew the jinn were more vulnerable in the dream world. *I could threaten her and force her to take me there.* Amanda paused the steady rhythm of her nails on the wood. *That could backfire, and I could end up being the one in trouble.*

Jinn had other weak points such as the iron-infused bracelets that still held Jacqueline hostage in the castle. But real torture. Amanda shook her head and closed her eyes. This jinni just wasn't afraid of her, or she was afraid of something much worse. *Maybe I need to up the stakes in a different way.* She thought of the young woman, Kiami, her unknowing host from the vision she had recognized Jacqueline in. Amanda had felt something familial between them, and the way Kiami had spoken to the jinni, as if she had expected a different reaction from her entirely.

The excitement of the realization gave her renewed energy. The chair toppled over as Amanda pushed it back and stood; maybe mentioning her name to the jinni would be enough to get her talking.

She treaded lightly down the dark stone staircase that led into the dungeon. She still held out hope that despite the fact she had brought Jacqueline to the castle forcefully, she would help. But as the rock wall shifted out of her way to allow her access to her prisoner, the demeanor of the waiting jinni spoke otherwise.

She stood with her hands planted firmly on each hip, staring at Amanda. A flame danced in the irises of her yellow eyes, a sign that Amanda had come to realize meant extreme anger. She had only seen such a flame dancing in Aden's irises twice: once while they had both still been prisoners of Jacob, and again on the day she had kidnapped Jacqueline.

Amanda tried to keep her voice light as she spoke. "Would you like anything to eat?"

"I have grown so tired of your questions," Jacqueline snapped. "I have said all I can say."

Amanda dropped her smile and mirrored the stance of the jinni. "Your answers have all been nonsense. I mean, I'm sure they mean something; don't get me wrong, but it seems as if you really wanted me to stop whatever this thing is, I wouldn't have to force information out of you." Her face grew warm with anger as she stared back at her unflinching captive. The gem in her pocket seemed to hum with energy. Amanda lowered her arms and took a deep breath. She didn't remember putting it there before her descent into the dungeon. She released the breath slowly as she stepped closer to Jacqueline. Letting her anger get the best of her was not going to help.

She lowered herself onto the cold stone floor and motioned for the jinni to join her. "Let's review what we know and see if it sparks anything new." Amanda shifted herself to cross her legs. "First, I will apologize. I am sorry that I lost my temper." She threw a quick smile at the jinni. "That day we finally found that you had returned to the tomb, we had been searching for so long, and I guess it didn't help matters that you immediately bound yourself by some spell that would make you unable to answer questions."

The jinni opened her mouth but hesitated, as if trying to test the words before speaking. "Any jinni could know that there is only one way for someone like me not to be seen by someone like you. You used jinni blood."

Amanda waved her words away. "I had thought of that, but it just didn't add up." She shook her head. "No, you were already casting the spell before we approached you."

The jinni looked up again, and Amanda held up her hand to stop her from speaking. "Which leads me to believe you were trying to stop someone else from asking you questions."

The jinni's eyes were trained on Amanda, but she didn't speak. Her yellow eyes glowed, but the flame no longer wavered in her irises.

Amanda reached up and smoothed her hair back. "You said some hurtful things to me that day, Jacqueline, and I deserve an explanation."

"You have demon blood."

"Only half and does that really make me an... what was that you called me? An abomination? A year ago, I didn't even know of my mother's true heritage, and I doubt a woman I have never met has had any influence on me."

The jinni closed her eyes and shook her head. "I can't."

Amanda pounded her fist on the floor. "Well then, tell me who can. Or should I listen to the green-haired creature that invades my dreams every night?"

The jinni looked back up at her, eyes wide.

Am I finally getting somewhere? "Who is he, and what does he really want, Jacqueline?"

The jinni lowered her head and stared down at the floor.

"Fine." Amanda hopped up. "He told me not to trust you." She turned to make her way back through the opening and then turned back. "Maybe Kiami will be more helpful."

Jacqueline was in front of her before her eyes even had time to register the jinni's movement. "How do you know about her? Did he tell you?"

Amanda looked down at her. *She doesn't know about the visions. That's one question answered.* "You haven't answered my question about the monster." She yanked her arms lose and folded them in front of her.

"The creature, your monster, is the master of the realm of chaos — Abaddon." The jinni reached out toward Amanda again. This time, she stepped back before she could get a hold of her arm. A haunted look had filled Jacqueline's eyes and she glanced around the room, as if searching for a spy. Her voice was only a whisper as she continued. "If he can reach your dreams here in the Arcane realm, then he can affect things in the Human realm." Her lip quivered as she finished.

"How do I know I can believe you, Jacqueline? How can I be

sure that he isn't telling the truth? I have never even heard of the Chaos realm."

"I can't tell you what you need to hear."

Amanda clicked her tongue. "That's a pity. I thought we were making real progress." She turned back on her heel in the direction of the doorway as the jinni spoke again.

"Wait," Jacqueline pleaded, "just wait."

The jinni looked frazzled as Amanda turned back to her. "You said you have never heard of the Chaos realm. Do you know the story of our world?"

"What does a myth have to do with anything?"

"The stories hold pieces of truth. If you really want to understand the things I said to you, you need to listen."

Amanda leaned against the wall by the doorway and dropped her arms back to her sides. "Fine, then, go on with your story."

The jinni cleared her throat. "I haven't recited the origin of Sumir in a long time, so bear with me."

"Sumir?"

The jinni lowered herself back to the floor, and Amanda couldn't help but wonder why she refused to use the furniture Amanda had Aden bring down for her. It was a luxury she wasn't given when she was a captive here.

"Sumir is what the jinn call this planet. All the races did at one time..." The last word seemed to stick in her throat, and she let out a strangled cough before continuing. "A world that was created by wrath." The jinni paused as Amanda began to move toward her to take a place on the floor nearby. As she, sat she motioned for Jacqueline to continue.

"In the beginning, our universe was a great empty void. This void, it is said, contained space for endless worlds. One day, out of the void, emerged two powerful celestial beings, Eaki and

Aya. They had traveled from another universe in search of a place where there was room for their godlike children to grow. They had brought with them the knowledge of creation and set about molding a simple world to live together in the center of the universe.

"One by one, as their children were born, they raised them to adolescence. Knowing that at this age, their children would begin to become restless and crave a deeper purpose, they sent them out into this universe to create a single world of their own to cultivate and control. They were each given a limited number of enchanted supplies to use. That is how our sun, our moons, and each unique planet came into existence."

Amanda recalled the myth she had read in the library when she was still a prisoner of Jacob. Some of the delicate pages had been torn from the book, and she had dismissed the tale as another one of his tricks. She couldn't help but wonder if the jinni was tricking her now. Abaddon had warned her that Jacqueline would never trust someone with demon blood coursing through her veins.

A loud yawn forced her mouth open, and the jinni shot her a sharp look. "Promise me you're not going to keep interrupting."

"I think I have heard this one before."

The jinn held her hand out. "Promise, or I won't continue."

Amanda rolled her eyes and accepted her hand. "I promise no more interruptions."

The jinn didn't let go. "Or questions."

Amanda gave her hand a firm shake. "Or questions."

The jinni smiled. "Good, now let's continue... So it went until Aya gave birth to triplet daughters: Sophia, the firstborn, Akila, the middle daughter, and Mia, the youngest. The two younger siblings bickered constantly and fought for their parents' attention. As the girls neared adolescence, their competitive nature only grew worse.

"Sophia overheard Eaki and Aya discussing her two younger sisters and was troubled to hear that they doubted the girls would be able to sustain their creations for long. When the time came, Eaki gave them each a chunk of enchanted clay, seeds, and some drops of his celestial blood. He then sent them into the universe to create their individual worlds.

"Sophia followed her sisters, and watching them bicker and fight, she decided that they could not be trusted to fulfill their father's wishes. Determined to help them succeed and make her father proud, she persuaded them to combine the resources to create one larger, more diverse world together so they could share equally in the responsibilities.

"Akila and Mia eagerly handed over the halves of their clay that were meant to be the basis for their three small worlds. Sophia lumped the pieces of clay together and carefully started to shape the world. As she worked, the younger sisters teased and tormented one another.

"Sophia borrowed inspiration for many of her designs in this new world from stories her parents had told her of their favorite planet in the distant universe they had come from. She created a flat mass of land and surrounded it with water. She molded rivers, mountains, and valleys. When everything seemed to be balanced, she shook the remaining tiny flecks of clay from her hands, creating small stars in orbit around the world.

"Satisfied that she had included everything required for obtaining harmony, she went to work molding a race of humans. Sophia carefully considered every little detail before applying the final touches and bringing them to life. To her, free will was the only real gift they needed to thrive.

"Sophia was content with the intelligent beings that she created and enjoyed watching them learn and progress. Mia and Akila also watched the humans. Although the humans were quite intelligent, they appeared weak to Mia and Akila. The sisters decided they would each make a magical race and have a contest between them to decide which of the two could create the most powerful beings.

"Akila created the elemental spirits, the jinn, born of smokeless fire.

"In response, Mia created beings with great arcane magic and taught them to hate the jinn and to pursue them relentlessly.

"As the two races fought one another, Sophia's race of humans was often caught in the middle. Not having natural magic themselves, they were unable to put up an adequate defense. Sophia couldn't bear to see her humans so abused, so she jumped down onto the plate of land, splitting it into several pieces and spreading them apart across the great seas that she had created. Hoping to spare her human race from future devastation, she placed them all onto one of the masses of land.

"Akila and Mia continued to pit their creations against one another, but it became clear that the two species were somewhat equally matched. Still, craving victory, Akila used the last of her clay to create beings of pure light and energy.

"In response, Mia created demons of pure darkness, able to harness the shadows.

"Again the sisters sent their creations on a path of destruction. By this time, all being intelligent and curious species, they had discovered various ways to travel the great seas. Once again, humans were thrust into a war they had no chance of surviving. Sophia scolded her sisters for being so careless as she watched her humans brought to the brink of extinction.

"Still, the sisters ignored Sophia's plea to stop their ruthless campaign. The battles raged on until only two humans remained. Sophia's anger grew, and she was filled with rage at the destruction of the creations that she had worked so hard on. She ripped and shredded the very fabric of the world, tearing each species away from the others and separating them into five different planes, with the humans in the centermost realm.

"Once these changes were made, Sophia knew they could not be undone. Still disgusted with her sisters, she created two more planes; the realm of the goddess was set above all of the other planes. She forbade her sisters from joining her there.

"Into the seventh plane she threw her remaining ingredients at random. Sophia then ordered her sisters to live in that realm of chaos far below the other planes. Only then did her younger siblings stop bickering amongst themselves. Seeing what had befallen their world, the two younger sisters felt guilty and longed to earn back Sophia's favor.

"Akila and Mia still had a few supplies remaining, seven drops of creator's blood and seven seeds from the sacred tree. Akila took the tree seeds and put them in each new plane that had been created, connecting them once again in secret locations that would allow passage from plane to plane.

"Mia created seven powerful gems to represent each of the planes and offered the stones to Sophia as penance.

"Sophia had missed her sisters and was impressed by their gifts. She allowed them to remain with her in the realm of the goddess to help watch over the original five realms.

"As time went by, the creatures below in the seventh realm were all but forgotten. Left unchecked to mature and evolve on their own without the guidance of the goddesses, they became loathsome and villainous.

"Some of the beings blamed the humans' existence on the sep-aration of their planes and were deeply resentful. Others missed the humans, especially the jinn, and passed the knowledge of what had happened down through the generations.

"Most humans forgot about magic altogether."

Amanda watched as Jacqueline stood up and brushed herself off. She finally had a name to put to her nighttime tormentor's face, but what good would it do, and how much did she trust this jinni? For all she knew, Jacqueline could have altered the myth to her advantage at any point. She remained seated, still trying to digest the story. The only things mentioned that seemed to hold any clue was the bit about the gifts that the sisters used to appease Sophia. She wondered if they were in some way related to the rune-carved trees that she had encountered in the past. *Could they be the very same trees mentioned?*

Jacqueline spoke again as Amanda approached her, ready with a batch of fresh questions. "A thing created by wrath will no doubt come to an end in a similar way." She had moved over to the far wall and seemed to be staring up at nothing in particular.

It wasn't until Amanda attempted to reply that she realized the jinni had tricked her again. She grunted as she tried to force the questions out of her mouth, but her face grew warmer with each passing second.

Annoyed with herself just as much as with Jacqueline, she turned on her heels and made a hasty retreat before she could do something she would regret.

5

Emily - Dumpster Diving

By the time Emily noticed the sign lingering above the treetops, she had thought of a plan of sorts.

The metal sign glowed a single red neon word: Diner. As Emily got closer, she could see that it was actually much more. Besides the long, white, rectangular building that served as the restaurant, there was a smaller white building that not only claimed to have restrooms with lockers, but actual showers with hot water. Emily was thrilled at the thought, but it would have to wait for now.

Picnic tables were lined up in between the buildings so patrons could eat or relax outside before returning to the road. A few small metal charcoal grills were cemented into the ground near them.

The large, circular driveway had all types of vehicles parked in it: cars packed to the gills, campers, large supply trucks. There was even a big gas service area for refueling. This was obviously a popular rest stop for many types of people.

Emily continued slowly and deliberately around the property, as if she were stretching her legs after a long car ride. She found what she was looking for a short way off from the main path, enclosed on three sides and the top by high brown wooden fencing. The smell hit her while she was still several yards away and continued to intensify as she moved closer. She wanted to turn around, but she knew it was her best chance at finding what she was looking for.

Flies swarmed around the top of the mountain of trash. Identical plastic bags were piled high above the rim of the dumpster. She peeked out from around the fencing; she hadn't been able to think of any plausible excuse for what she was about to do if someone happened to come by with a fresh load of trash.

She yanked on one of the bags, hard, and stepped back away as far as she could as several bags tumbled down to the ground. One split along the side as it made impact directly in front of her, displaying a mass of decomposing leftovers. Emily covered her mouth with her hand as she gagged and dry-heaved at the sight of the maggots squirming about in a frenzy over the sudden intrusion of light.

Gulping, she stepped over the bag and its spilled contents to peer into the dumpster. Two bags had been uncovered that did not match the rest, trash that had been tossed in by patrons trying to empty their vehicles before heading back out onto the road.

Emily reached for the smaller bags, holding her breath as she pulled them up and out. She carried the bags behind the dumpster, where the wall and the dumpster itself would block her from anyone's immediate view. She dumped the contents of the first bag: empty cans, bottles and chip wrappers, nothing that would be useful to her. She sighed and emptied the second bag.

This one's contents were much more diverse. The sight of a wad of used tissues gave her pause. She used an empty chip bag from the first pile to cover her hand while she inspected the contents more thoroughly. It was a clunky solution, but it would help her avoid direct contact. A torn bra, a discarded wallet, ripped on the side and completely emptied of its contents, an aluminum can that had been emptied and refilled again by cigarette butts, a discarded cell phone with a cracked screen. She picked it up to inspect it. The battery had been removed, but if she cupped it in her hand just so, no one would notice.

Emily placed it inside an empty chip bag, not wanting to touch it directly until she had a chance to wash it off. She rolled the chip bag around it and slid it into the top of her backpack. The sun was fading as she attempted to clean the mess up. She refilled the two bags and tossed them back up into the pile.

With a pang of guilt, she carefully pulled the torn bag to the side of the dumpster, trying not to rip it further. It was much harder to heft the larger bags back up over the rim. Sweat trickled from her forehead as she piled the remaining bags as neatly as she could.

Emily made her way to the bathroom. The yellow glow of the lights was calling to her. It would be fully dark soon, and she wanted to clean herself as best she could and take refuge inside the diner. She scurried past several parked cars. Several beach towels hung from the awning that had been rolled open along the side of a parked RV, no doubt an attempt to let them dry and avoid the musty, pungent smell of dampness from invading the campers' temporary home.

She thought of the pool. She had left her towel in the rush to get out of there, rolled up at the bottom of the chair she had been lounging in.

No lights were on inside the vehicle. Emily glanced around the parking lot. It seemed deserted, other than a few people that slept in their cars. She grabbed at one of the towels and held it tightly against her as she continued to the bathroom.

It took her eyes a moment to adjust to the harsh yellow lights inside. Someone was singing in one of the shower stalls as the water rained down. She placed her backpack on the floor by the sink stations and removed the broken phone. Taking a wad of paper towels and a few squirts of soap, she scrubbed at it until she was sure it was sanitized enough.

She moved to an empty shower stall, hanging her backpack on a hook behind the door. There was a thin plastic lining that split the area in half to protect dry items from the shower spray. Emily heard the water sputter in the other stall.

"Shoot" a woman exclaimed as she heard change clink to the ground. A loose quarter rolled under the stall and hit Emily in the foot. Emily leaned down and picked up the quarter, frowning. Disappointed, she inspected the shower. Sure enough, she saw a slot to insert coins. *Fifty cents for fifteen minutes*, the small plaque read. She only had singles left.

The water came back on in the other stall, and the woman clapped with joy, no doubt thinking she was alone in the bathroom.

Emily sat in the stall until she heard the wooden door bang shut behind her as she exited. She searched the floor for another dropped coin, with no luck. She washed up using the sink as best she could and headed to the diner.

The hot cup warmed her hands as she sat at one of the diner's small, round tables. It wasn't cold outside, but a chill ran through her. Emily couldn't believe she had gone through that dumpster. By some miracle, she had found what she needed. It was cracked, but she wouldn't let anyone examine it that closely.

Now, she just needed to find the right kind of family. She stared into the mug of dark liquid. It tasted bitter; she had never tried coffee before. She had never had the inclination to do so. She didn't hate it, at least, and it seemed to settle her stomach after her encounter.

Emily had studied the map that was still laid out in front of her. She had a feeling of the direction she needed to go in, though no real place to land. She chose a town almost at random and added it to the story she was building in her head.

She saw them sit down by the window: a young couple and a toddler. They were obviously taking a road trip and needed a rest. The disheveled woman disappeared into the bathroom and came back with freshly combed hair and a renewed spark in her eyes. Emily wished she had more than the change of clothing from the pool. The child was kicking his legs, wound up as if straight sugar had been his diet for the last few hours, a sure sign of being stuck in a car on a long road trip.

Just as the waitress brought the family the check, Emily picked up the cell phone and held it to her ear.

"Mom!" she exclaimed with all the enthusiasm she could muster. "Mom, slow down, are you okay? Breathe and take it one word at a time." She paused as if listening to a reply. She slatted her eyes and sighed. "Mom, I'm sorry, my bus won't leave for hours yet; I'm trying to hurry." She tried to sound as concerned as possible and rubbed her eyes with her free hand, trying to redden them just enough. She slumped forward as if distraught and in discomfort from her situation. "I'm sorry, just hold on." She made her voice crack at the end. "Love you too." She slipped the phone into her backpack so no one would see that it was off and buried her face in her arms on the tabletop, as if overcome with distress.

Emily could hear the concerned couple chattering away in hushed tones but didn't dare to look up. Just as Emily was about to lose her nerve and leave, she felt a gentle touch on her sleeve.

"I'm sorry to bother you, but are you all right?" the mother said, lowering herself into the empty seat in front of Emily. The woman's eyes wandered from Emily to the cup, and then to the map. She paused a moment as she inspected the lines and dots Emily had drawn before again returning to Emily's face.

Emily heard real concern in her voice and felt guilty for the ruse. Her stomach knotted uncomfortably before she even repeated the lie she had rehearsed. As she opened her mouth to respond, the woman interrupted with a gasp. "Oh, you poor thing. Come with us; we will give you a ride." She placed a reassuring hand over Emily's. "I'm Jill, my husband over there wrestling with the toddler is Jack, and the cute bug he's wrestling is Toby. We couldn't help but overhear what seemed to be a private and very distressing phone call for y'all. We are just passing through, and from the notes on your map it looks like we are going in the same direction."

"Emily," she said as she offered her hand to Jill. "No, I couldn't impose on your family like that." Emily wiped her face on her sleeve as Jill shook her other hand.

"Nonsense, we are going in that direction anyway!" the woman exclaimed with such enthusiasm that Emily wondered if she could really hold up her story once she got in the car. "It's no burden," she added loudly enough for her husband to hear. He responded by shooting Emily a tired half smile as he helped his son out of his seat. "Come on now. Did you take care of your check?" Emily nodded in response and followed them out to their car. "Lucky you that we were in that restaurant when you were." Jill opened the back passenger door and motioned for Emily to sit.

The vehicle carried the scent of chocolate and Play-Doh. "Yes, thank you." Emily watched out the window as the car pulled away from the parking lot. "So, are you guys from the south?" she asked, trying to be polite.

"Oh..." Jill giggled. "I am, or used to be, but my husband is from way up north. My accent makes everyone ask. How about you?"

"We moved around a lot," Emily said. *Better to keep it simple so I don't falter.*

"You must be worried sick about your momma. You look tired too. Completely drained, I'd say. There's a blanket in the seat behind you. Why don't you use it to cover up and try to get some rest while Jack drives."

Emily didn't bother to protest. It would be better if she did less talking anyway. She reached around awkwardly behind her and grasped at the blanket. It looked like a homemade quilt, and Emily felt almost safe for the first time in days as she wrapped it around herself and closed her eyes managing to mutter, "Thank you." Sleep came swiftly. Although she woke with a stiff neck, she had the most peaceful sleep she had since her hasty retreat from the pool. She felt refreshed.

She moved her head side to side to loosen the tight muscles, looked at the grinning toddler on her right, and smiled. He eyed her sheepishly, and she couldn't help but giggle at his chocolate-smeared face and purple goggles. They looked just like hers.

On the floor, the few contents of Emily's backpack spilled out, and she gasped, suddenly concerned that he had been playing with the broken phone. She didn't want her chauffeurs to realize it was not a working phone; it would ruin everything.

"Hey, did you get in my bag?" Emily asked, trying to sound light-hearted as she put her flip-flops away. "You can keep those." She gestured to the goggles. "I don't mind, but you shouldn't get in other people's stuff."

His mother turned around to scowl at him. "Toby!"

He reached down and grabbed the amethyst before Emily could stop him; she hadn't anticipated his quick lunge. Before she could do anything, he let out a bloodcurdling scream and dropped the gem. His father was so startled that he slammed on the brakes, and the car skidded along the side of the road. The tires kicked up a cloud of dust as the car fought to stop.

Toby was shaking his hand as if it still hurt, and tears streamed from his face. Emily's eyes widened. *Did this ever happen before?* His hand was blistering as if burned. *No one other than me had ever had an opportunity to pick up the stone before.* There was a frenzy of movement as his parents removed him from the car. Emily put the stone away quickly as she exited the vehicle.

Jill's nostrils flared. "What did you do?" she screamed at Emily. Her face was red with anger. *Showing them the stone will just make it worse.* Jack pushed Emily away from them as they examined Toby's hand. Emily didn't know how to defend herself; she couldn't explain the stone to them. Ashamed, she looked at her feet and allowed them to throw a barrage of only half intelligible accusations at her.

Awkwardly, she stood there listening as they patched Toby's hand up with burn cream and a bandage from the first-aid kit that had been in the back. As Jill helped her son back into the car, still wiping away his tears as they flowed and placing kisses on his forehead to soothe him, Jack turned to Emily. His eyes were narrowed, and his brow was furrowed. Emily took a step back.

"What did you do to my son?" Emily shook her head side to side, too afraid to try to speak. "Tell me!" he yelled, spit flying from his mouth.

"Nothing," Emily whispered, again looking at her feet. *I didn't, though,* she realized and raised her eyes to his. "I didn't do anything to him." He turned back to the car and tossed her backpack out beside her.

"Jack!" Jill gasped. "You can't just abandon her here."

"The hell I can't," he spat as he got into the driver's seat. "I knew there was something not right with her the moment I laid eyes on her. Who puts streaks of purple in their hair?" He pointed out the door at Emily as he ranted. "But no, you have to do your good deed for the day."

"But Jack, she would have been safer at the diner," Jill stammered. "We can't just abandon her." She turned toward Emily; her face had totally drained of color.

"She's not getting back in this car!" He turned the key and the car roared to life.

"Maybe we should at least take her to the next town," Jill urged, grabbing at his arm as he placed his hands on the steering wheel.

Emily, not wanting to cause any more damage, tapped on the window, shaking her head. "No." She wiped her tear stained face. "I will be fine." *How much farther can the next town really be anyway?*

"We can't just leave you." Jill's eyes glistened with tears.

"Go," Emily insisted. "I'm good. I don't want to put anyone in danger."

"I'm sorry." Jill peered out the window.

Emily gave her a thumbs-up and stepped away from the car. She started walking even before the family moved to pull away. *Maybe I should have just told them the truth from the beginning.* Emily shook her head. *They wouldn't have believed me.*

6

Emily - Town Limits

Emily's legs ached. The setting sun was glowing orange in the distance. She felt filthy, run-down and thirsty. She regretted tossing out her empty water bottle. Her eyes were heavy.

Emily had been walking blindly. *For how long?*

Confused, she turned in a circle, exploring the terrain. She was startled by the change in her surroundings.

How could everything have shifted so significantly without me noticing?

Emily's mind had been wandering from the incident with John Doe to Vanessa and the bird...

The ground under her feet was neither rich black pavement nor the thick green grass she was expecting to see. Her shoes were covered in the same layer of dusty brown earth that stretched out beneath her. An unpaved road twisted out into the distance.

Back in the direction she had come from, she could just barely see the lights of some scattered houses. Emily squinted her eyes at them.

I don't remember walking by any houses. She crinkled her nose.

There was nothing here except a rough wooden sign that had the words *Town Limits* carved out on it.

Town limits? What town? She made another circle. *There's nothing here.*

Emily tried to sit with her back propped up against the narrow signpost. Her muscles screamed, even in a resting position. She couldn't seem to get comfortable or content. She tried lying, kneeling ... resting her head on her backpack. She even tried to close her eyes and hum a song. Her mind wouldn't stop working. Even though her muscles felt like jelly, something nagged at her to move.

Emily opened her eyes to see a blue wisp floating above her. She frowned. "What?" She covered her face with her arm. "What?" she yelled. "I don't know what you want me to do!" Every decision she made seemed to be wrong.

The blue wisp circled slowly around her, then moved a few feet farther away from the dirt road. Emily stared after the specter, expecting it to disappear into the distance.

When she didn't budge, it repeated the action again. "Okay," she whispered, putting her hands on the ground to help push herself to her feet. Her sore body protested, causing her to stumble as she tried to stand.

The wisp moved forward and stopped, waiting until Emily followed, then continued on toward what looked like an empty, dried-up field. She tried to keep up with the blue creature as it darted ahead, *one foot in front of the other.* She had to concentrate on her feet to keep them moving forward.

The wisp circled back and returned to her side as she fell to her knees on the cracked, dust-covered ground.

In front of her, a stream shimmered like a mirage. Emily listened to the water gurgle and splash as it flowed off into the distance.

She reached forward, skimming the surface with her fingers

before plunging them into the cool liquid and splashing her face with it. She cupped her hand and sipped as she took in the eerie scene in front of her.

It was one of the strangest things she had ever laid eyes on.

On the dehydrated side where she knelt, everything was dried and shriveled as if the water could not penetrate the earth. Yet on the other bank, merely three feet in front of her, a thick blanket of grass covered the ground, and flowers dotted the landscape. Emily dipped her hand back in to take another sip of the refreshing water.

Her eyes, still searching as she drank, rested on a tree that grew close to the shallow bank on the other side. It was full of leaves, with the exception of the one barren branch that protruded out over the water's edge. The otherwise healthy brown bark was missing from this portion that appeared to be struggling to survive on this side of the stream.

Maybe I have had enough. Emily dried her hand on her shirt as she stood. *Where did that wisp go?*

She peered across the field. The uncut grass bent and moved as if blown about by the wind. She licked her index finger and held her arm out. Nothing. *What wind?* The air was humid and thick; there wasn't the slightest hint of a breeze on her skin.

She crossed her arms and stared ahead, not believing what her eyes were seeing but unable to look away from the oddity. *Impossible.*

Emily took a step back from the water's edge just as the wisp reappeared from somewhere deeper in the field and headed in a straight line toward her. Emily cocked her head at the specter as it neared. "If you think I'm walking through this weird stream, you're crazy." She shook her head and turned her back. The wisp appeared directly in front of her. "No." She dropped her arms and turned back toward the stream. The wisp circled back into her vision. Emily stomped her foot and again turned toward the barren landscape that seemed to stretch before her for miles.

She closed her eyes. She couldn't think with the wisp darting around her head. *Maybe it's not that side there is something wrong with, but this one. At least over there everything is healthy and alive.*

Emily pushed her fingers through her hair and let out a breath as she opened her eyes. Two wisps now hovered in front of her. She moved back to the water's edge and sat with a huff, pulling off her sneakers one at a time and placing them down beside her backpack.

Dipping one toe in with her other foot planted firmly on the ground behind her, she again felt the cool water rush over her skin. She inched forward until her foot was completely submerged. The bottom felt as smooth as glass, as if it were covered with the perfectly polished pebbles of a walkway.

Emily pulled her foot back out and sat to examine it, pinching each toe and checking each nail as though they might fall off from the submersion. She stood and turned to her backpack. Her shoes were not where she had left them.

The wisps... "Really, guys?" She shouldered her bag and turned toward the stream. "That was not necessary." She stared ahead at her shoes and the pair of wisps that hovered above them across the water. Emily placed her hands on her hips, "I was going to go. I was just ... preparing."

The wisps remained where they were as Emily let out a sigh. "Okay, I'm coming." *I will just cross as fast as possible.* She placed one foot back into the stream and held her breath as she waded across, not releasing it until she reached the other side. Again she examined herself as she breathed in the fresher air.

Life surrounded her on this side; she could smell the flowers, birds chirped, and insects buzzed. It was like she had stepped into another world.

The wisps darted out of her path as she reached for her shoes. "See." Emily scrunched her brow. "Don't do that again." She slipped her feet into her sneakers and looked out into the field. The wisps had vanished again. "Now what?" she called out. "Forward march, I guess."

Darkness was beginning to creep in around Emily as she trudged on through the field.

She could see lights up ahead in the distance. *A town?* Emily squinted, unable to distinguish the outline of any buildings. "I can do this," she breathed as she pushed herself to move forward.

The field ended abruptly. Emily stopped with her sneakers pressed against the edge of a sidewalk. She looked around cautiously, reluctant to move another step. The town was still and silent. *How late is it?* Streetlights seemed few and far in between, emitting only the lightest yellow glow. A blur of movement caught her eye. A street lamp illuminated a dark green bench; wisps swirled and danced around it. *Is it a warning? Or are they pleading with me to move forward?* Emily stepped onto the sidewalk and made her way across a paved street toward the wisps.

The wisps stopped their erratic movements as she removed her backpack and plopped down hard onto the bench, yawning. "Happy?" she whispered. "Good."

From her new seat, Emily could see the brick facade of several small unlit storefronts. She covered her mouth as she released another involuntary yawn. She pushed her backpack to the end of the seat and lay down with her head resting on it. The blue glow of the remaining wisps comforted her. Her eyes were already closed as she muttered, "You keep watch." Emily released a low giggle, knowing full well the wisps would be gone before she awoke, but was too exhausted to think about it.

7

Amanda - Hard Release

Amanda's eyes shot open. Large, round eyes stared straight into hers. Only they weren't her eyes at all; she was just a passenger unable to do anything but watch.

Her host's body jerked upright into a sitting position, and tight black spirals of hair sprang into Amanda's line of sight. She could feel the girl's heart thudding in her chest at the sight before her, but Amanda didn't feel fear coming from the girl.

Cautiously, her host took in the friendly brown eyes that greeted her own. The animal's mouth hung open, panting, tongue dripping as it dangled.

Amanda couldn't help but think the dog seemed to almost be smiling. His long, flowing coat was a golden hue, shimmering in the morning light.

Her host's heart rate slowed and her view shifted. She could see that the feet of her host were clad in sneakers, one with a blue shoelace and one with red.

Emily?

The memory of her first vision raced through her mind. She had almost forgotten about Emily and the day she had been thrust behind her eyes. *She wears her laces purposely mismatched in this way.*

When she had seen her open the box and reach in for the amethyst gem, she had felt the power in the stone, just as she had felt something when Erol first gave her the black diamond.

Still a prisoner of the sorcerer, Amanda remembered the helplessness she felt as she watched the events of the then eleven-year-old's birthday unfold — the girl's dismay at finding the injured bird and her sudden excitement at knowing she could do something about it.

She had only been a child doing what she thought was right, and Amanda had no way to warn her that there would be consequences. How quickly her happiness had dissolved after using the magic.

Amanda thought of the other visions she had been subjected to since then and the people in them. No other had affected her so much. She pushed the memory of the events away; she needed to pay attention if she was ever going to find a connection between the visions.

Her host looked around slowly, as if taking in her surroundings for the first time, just as Amanda was.

To her it looked as though she was at the very center of a dartboard. The town square where she stood harbored the life-size statue of a tree in its center. Carved limbs reached up and out at clumsy awkward angles. Unable to move closer to take in the full details of the representation, Amanda wondered what, if anything, she would find carved into its base if she were able to get a better look. A green blanket of manicured grass spread out from beneath the statue, ending at the sidewalk's edge.

From here it looked as though only one paved road led in and out of the quaint town; it looped around the center and then disappeared into the tree line beyond her immediate view. Several people strolled leisurely past the girl and into the businesses across the street, but apart from the dog, no one seemed to be worried that Emily had been asleep on the bench.

Amanda couldn't help but notice the lack of noise. Life seemed to move at a slower pace here, compared to the burg where she had once lived, and Emily seemed almost content to watch the town and its occupants as they strolled past, stopping to great one another.

Is she also afraid to move from her seat?

The sensation of a slobbery lick from the dog on her host's hand broke her train of thought, and as her view returned to the canine, Emily's emotions began to seem chaotic. Amanda felt like she was at the center of a giant knotted ball of yarn.

She doesn't want to disrupt the peaceful vision in front of her. Yet she wishes she was a part of it.

Emily's chest felt tight as Amanda tried to visualize herself unknotting the mess of conflicting thoughts and feelings, trying to make sense of the rush of information.

... Afraid her presence will put an end to the tranquility she sees now, Emily believes she will put them in danger from the moment she intervenes in their lives.

Is she scared of the people here or for them?

Could someone be hunting for her too?

"Shoo," her host breathed as she jumped to her feet. Emily had something clutched against her chest. Amanda watched as the dog cocked its head and barked, thumping his tail on the sidewalk. "Shoo now." With one quick movement, the dog sprang up onto its hind legs and lunged at the thing in Emily's arm, ripping it free.

With the red backpack in its mouth, it turned and bolted across the street. "HEY!"

As Emily followed the dog with her eyes, Amanda could see several businesses lined that side of the street, each with an almost identical awning stretched out above their doorways. The brick exteriors connected, creating a neat row. The dog ran through an open shop door and her host, Emily, raced across the street after the thief.

"You're late." The voice was not directed at Emily but at the dog, and she stared through Emily's eyes as the dog slunk through another doorway and out of sight. The woman behind the counter turned around, a sheepish grin plastered on her face. She seemed to be studying Emily before she bent down to lift up the hostage backpack from the floor near her feet. "Ah, this must be yours." There was a mischievous twinkle in her eye as she reached out to hand it to Emily.

"Thanks." The girl's heart thumped loudly against her chest, and Amanda wondered why she was so nervous. Emily fumbled as she reached for her backpack, and Amanda felt her instant relief as the strap was grasped in her fingers. To Amanda, the woman looked like the kind aunt she never had. The one that would send balloons to school so everyone would know it was your birthday or show up on the last day as a surprise to take you for ice cream.

The woman reached forward again, offering her hand. "I'm Gemma."

Gemma's hand felt warm in her host's as she accepted it, giving it one firm shake. "Emily." She smiled and glanced around. The front of the store was sparsely furnished. A few chairs were pushed up against one wall, and the counter where Gemma stood ran down the middle. A stack of magazines rested on one end, and a register stood on the other.

"Forgive me for being so forward, but you look a little lost and a bit exhausted. Have you only just arrived in town? We don't see too many new faces out here in the middle of nowhere, and once a mom, always a mom, ya know?"

Amanda thought she could feel the blood drain from the girl's face as she nodded in an uneasy response and bit painfully into her lower lip.

I should have tried to find her...

Gemma frowned and walked around the register. "I'm sorry, being from a small town like this, you forget that the world can be an unfriendly place. I didn't mean to startle you. Let's start over." She reached out and grabbed Emily's hand, shaking it gently. "I'm Gemma, and it's nice to see a new friendly face around here. You must be wondering about the sign."

"The sign?"

Gemma raised her eyebrows and grinned. "Yes, the one in the window ... job's yours if you want to give it a go. We all need something to help tether us in place, and it seems you have a way with animals."

"You want to give me a job? We have only just met."

"Well, yes, why wouldn't I?" Gemma gave Emily a puzzled look. "You don't have to answer me now. Why don't you think on it and get back to me? You could spend a little time exploring our small community." She reached into her apron pocket and brought out a sealed envelope just as an anxious bark came from somewhere in the back. "Hold your horses!" She gazed back at Emily expectantly, and Amanda wondered what she was missing from the interaction. "Don't mind that old girl; she's just impatient to get her nails trimmed." Gemma held the envelope up for Emily. "As I said, we don't get many visitors, but if you take this note to Nina, she has a few rooms she rents out on occasion, and I'm sure she will be happy to help you out."

Emily reached for the envelope as the vision faded. Everything went dark, and Amanda waited for the sound of the waterfall to fill her ears. She felt a pang of guilt for not trying to help Emily after she had freed herself from the sorcerer.

As Amanda's eyes adjusted to the candlelit room, she turned in her chair to see Aden staring down at her.

"I don't suppose you're going to tell me what that was all about?"

Amanda sat back and pushed her hair out of her face. "No." She smiled slyly up at him. "We have more pressing matters to attend to." A book lay open in front of her, and she snapped it closed as Aden tried to get around her to take a better look.

"I need your help with something." Amanda studied his face. He hadn't been quite the same since she brought Jacqueline to the dungeon. "Are you ready to go?"

Aden narrowed his eyes. "More questioning? Aren't we beyond that?"

Amanda stood. "I can handle the jinni. I have a different errand for you."

"I don't want you to handle her, Amanda. I want you to let her go. When we went to find her, you didn't say anything about keeping her here against her will. In fact, I would think that would be the last thing you would want to do to someone."

Amanda gawked back at him. "What else would you have me do, given the circumstances? I went to her looking for answers. Instead she talks to me in riddles. How can I stop something if I don't know what it is? Besides, I am going to send her where she belongs. I just need her to tell me one more thing."

"When did you become so cold, so cruel? You need to stop looking for answers to be handed to you and start asking for assistance in finding them. I can help you."

"If anyone could understand, I would think it would be you. How many times have you played a part in things you couldn't control? You know what it's like to have the burden of people's lives hanging by a thread from your hands. It's awful. I didn't ask for this. I don't want to have to make these decisions! You were there, Aden. You heard what she said. If I don't fix this, everything tears apart. Do we just let that happen?"

"There has to be a better way. Please, Amanda. Don't do something you will regret."

Amanda looked him in the eye. "It's far too late for that, Aden. Maybe I shouldn't have tried in the first place. Maybe none of this would have happened."

"No, even if Jacob hadn't found you, you still would have been a part of it."

"But I would have been none the wiser about it, would I?" She lifted her hand and placed it on his shoulder. "There's a girl that can help me find answers, and I need you to bring her to me."

Aden stepped back from her touch. "How do you know where she is?"

"She's been looking for someone like you; she's just not looking in the right places. Her name is Kiami, and I have no doubt that you will know her when you see her."

She had gotten the impression from Jacqueline's actions that Kiami had no idea of her *friend's* true nature, and the unmethodical routine the young woman displayed in her searches helped to solidify her idea that the young woman knew absolutely nothing about the jinn.

Amanda picked the book up from the desk and carried it to the overflowing shelves that lined the wall. "Don't worry, Aden, I won't harm a hair on her pretty little head." She slipped the book into its place and pulled a folded map from the shelf. "Besides, you love spending time in the Human realm," she added, tossing the map to him.

With Aden occupied, she had to think about how she was going to get more from Jacqueline. But there was something about this last vision that wasn't sitting well with Amanda, and she replayed it in her head. She knew time moved faster in the arcane realm, but Emily was definitely no longer the helpless eleven-year-old she had first seen. Had Emily really grown so much?

Apart from her eye color, Amanda's outward appearance had hardly changed since she had been taken from the Human realm by the sorcerer. She and Aden had kept track of the days as they passed, it had been just about a human year's worth, but time moved differently in each of the realms.

When she had seen that innocent child open the box and reach in for the amethyst gem, she had felt it. The power in the stone, just as she had felt something when Erol had first given her the black diamond. Who had left the amethyst for Emily? And why hadn't she known about her ability when she touched it as Emily had?

Amanda couldn't control when the visions would come. She never knew what she was going to see. What did the people in her visions have in common? Nothing she could detect before. Some were male, some were female. They seemed to be spread out across the Human realm. Their families were all different, their gifts were all different. She hadn't thought about Emily's birthday in a long time. Was it only a coincidence that she and Emily both had a gem? Did the others? Could that be the thing connecting them, and were they the things causing the visions?

How can I ask about the visions or the gems without posing an actual question? She began to pace the room, still angry that she had allowed herself to be tricked again. She had been naive to think that the jinni didn't have something planned, the way she offered the story up after not making a peep for days in the dungeon. And Amanda had agreed willingly, like she was just going to give her the answers to everything. "Why did I shake her hand and agree?"

Jacqueline had taken advantage of the opportunity. Now every time Amanda tried to ask her a question, her mouth refused to open, and only grunts would make it out of her throat. As far as she knew, there was no way for her to reverse the spell on herself. She would never be able to ask Jacqueline another question, unless she reversed it, and that wasn't going to happen any time soon.

Amanda carried a single metal candelabra in her hand as she maneuvered down the narrow stone passageway. The heels of her boots made a tapping noise on the stairs.

At the bottom, she waved her hand in front of the wall and waited as the stones shifted into the shape of a door.

This time the jinni was kneeling on the floor, her waist-long hair hung in snarls around her face. Amanda plopped down on the cold stones beside her. She had thought over the things she wanted to say and worded them just so, in the hopes the jinni would understand and respond.

"I'm not going to ask why in the world you won't use the furniture I had set up down here. It's a lot better than what I had that's for sure... In fact, you made sure that I couldn't ask you anything at all, or so it would seem."

The jinni looked up at her with her unusual yellow eyes and crinkled her nose. "Interesting."

Amanda leaned back on the palms of her hands. "Well, I guess I should thank you for that anyway. There would have been no point to ask when you only answer me in riddles and myths."

She sat back up and sucked in her breath. "Anyway, I was thinking about the tomb and the things you said, and I had a sudden epiphany. You see, I have to forgive myself for not noticing sooner. As you know, I'm not getting much sleep.

"All this time, I thought you were picking your things up from the floor in the tomb, but you didn't bring anything with you here to the Arcane realm, nothing except the clothing on your back, anyway." The jinni didn't budge as Amanda hopped up from the floor, dusting herself off as she stood.

"I think you hid something in the tomb that day." She placed her hands firmly on each hip. "Which lead me to wonder why..."

The jinni's eyes grew wide, and her lips parted, but before she could utter a sound, Amanda began again. "Please don't interrupt! Anyway, where was I? So, how or why would you hide something in a place where lost things are found?" Amanda glared at the jinni. "Unless maybe you stole the thing to begin with."

Jacqueline sneered back up at Amanda as she began to pace back and forth in front of her hostage. "Yes it does sound crazy, I know, but it isn't, is it, because the only being that can go back and retrieve it now is the one that it rightly belongs to."

Amanda stopped in front of the jinni and leaned down with her hands on her knees, studying the jinni's eyes. "What's done is done, I guess." She stood back up to hover over Jacqueline. "I think you want to be here, but you know what? I have a guest coming, and she wouldn't like it if she knew I had someone in the dungeon. Whoever you are hiding from can have you. Stand up." She tugged at the jinni's arm.

"Before I remove these bracelets, you're going to read this spell and make it binding." Amanda pulled a wrinkled paper from her pocket and held it out for the jinni.

Jacqueline reached out for the ancient yellow page, wincing as she took it into her hand. "Why?" The jinni traced the drawn-on runes with her finger, her frown growing deeper as she studied them.

"Oh stop, you will be fine in the emerald mountains. Isn't it where jinn belong anyway? I think you have interfered sufficiently." Amanda bent down again and produced a pocket knife that had been wedged into the top of her boot.

"I said what I could." The usual mischievous twinkle was gone from Jacqueline's eyes, replaced by a look of dread.

Amanda flicked her wrist, causing the blade to open as she

grabbed the jinni's free hand. "It wasn't enough." She pressed the blade of the pocket knife into her flesh, until a small pool of blood formed in her palm. "Do it."

The jinni's cheeks burned red as she raised her hand and smashed it down onto the rune-covered page with such force that blood splattered and oozed along its surface. A few drops dripped onto the floor.

Amanda smiled back at her. "Now who's lost their temper."

The jinni remained silent as she dropped the paper and held out her hands.

Amanda slipped the bracelets from the jinni's wrists. "At least when it's all over we will know right where to find you."

The jinni squeezed her uncut hand into a fist and gritted her teeth as the magic began to pull her from the Arcane realm. To Amanda it looked as though she was trying to fight the magic that conspired to rip her away. As she disappeared from the room, her final words traveled back to Amanda's ears, not much more than a whisper. "Kiami is like you."

8

Kiami - Siren Song

The dance floor would have been completely black if not for the constant flash of the strobe lights. Music pounded in Kiami's chest as she studied the flailing bodies that moved all around her. She opened her mouth slightly, releasing a soft sound from her lips, a sound that at first only she could hear. She swayed to the calmer, quieter rhythm that came from somewhere deep within herself. As she sang, the mob calmed. Their movements slowed, as if the only song that penetrated their eardrums was the one emanating from her. These people would be willing to follow her anywhere if she asked.

As they moved in unison with her, she examined the room, searching for any one person that wasn't affected by her singing. When she was certain no such person was present, she quieted, releasing them from her enthrallment. The people stood momentarily stunned, looking at each other and muttering in confusion.

Kiami's cheeks burned as she hurried toward the exit, pushing her way past them and out into the night air.

As the doors swung shut behind her, she felt a hot tear roll down her cheek. She longed for companionship, but not like that.

She breathed in deeply and wiped the tear away. Her silver-flecked eyes locked onto the nearest alley. She walked toward it, craving the cover of full darkness for her change. Kiami was thankful that the magic of her transformation was swift.

She yearned for her mother's embrace and her aunt Jacqueline's affections. She had been too long now without anyone to talk to.

She perched atop a tall building, her gray and silver feathers rustling in the cool breeze, her large eyes watching the people as they came and went far below her. There had to be someone like them out there, anyone that was not affected by her influence, someone that could give her the companionship she needed. They had loved her for who she was, not because of what she was. Kiami stretched her wings and flew away from the city.

Lights twinkled along the skyline on one side of her while giant waves crashed into the large rocks below on the other. She followed the coastline back toward her home. The large, empty house rested high up in the cliffs above the beach and seemed to be held in place by massive stone formations on each side, which created a sort of separation, like it was two different worlds connected on the very edge of existence itself.

The once carefully maintained grounds were now a jungle of grass and weeds. With her heart broken, Jacqueline had dismissed the family's remaining employees almost immediately after the loss of Kiami's mother.

Everyone was aware of their eccentric behavior, so the dismissal came as no surprise. Many had been expecting to be replaced within months of being hired anyway, as it had become a custom for the woman of the house to do so on a regular basis. Only Kiami knew that they did it to protect her.

The lovingly tended house was now empty, except for growing layers of cobwebs and dust. She bypassed the front doors and entered through a vented skylight. She didn't land until reaching her bedroom.

Kiami watched in the mirror as she transformed back into a young woman. This too wasn't a gradual change but rather sudden, almost the blink of an eye. She wondered if there was a second where she stopped being in the room altogether.

Reflections are curious things, and Kiami inspected hers often, not because she was beautiful but because she felt there were answers hidden there, buried deep within.

She thought if she stared long and hard enough, the answers would come. Kiami studied every detail, from the depths of her eyes to the individual strands of her dark hair; every pore was part of her story, she just knew it.

All of her life, Kiami had been prone to sudden rapid growth spurts, and the fact that they had stopped so abruptly perplexed her. She was certain she looked the same as she did the day before and the month before that. She was worried that it wasn't normal, but nothing about her had ever been considered normal.

Time didn't move any more since her mother died. There were no more parties, no more shopping trips, no more adventures out to sea. Her mother had possessed a limitless curiosity about the world and wanted to explore every inch of it.

Kiami wanted her mom back, wanted to be held and told everything would be all right. She needed to feel love again. She wanted to confess about the young man and have her mother tell her how to stop it from happening again, but Kiami knew her mother was just as clueless about the things she could do. At least she would have had someone there beside her, someone holding her hand reassuringly, someone devoted and caring.

Kiami made her way down the hall, stopping in front of her mother's room. There was nothing left of her inside. Even the drapes had been ripped from the windows. Months had passed since Jacqueline had emptied it of her mother's belongings, but the sight still made Kiami feel hollow.

She continued down the hallway. She had stopped looking for signs of Jacqueline's return weeks ago and had not ventured into her room since the day Jacqueline found Kiami on the beach.

The door creaked open as she pushed through it, moving to the window that looked over the shore below. Her flowered tea set still sat where she had left it, the liquid long since evaporated, leaving light brown stains inside the cup.

Beyond the cliff's edge, Jacqueline had a clear view of the beach. A shiver ran through Kiami as she imagined what Jacqueline must have seen that day while she sat sipping her tea and watching the waves beat against the shore.

Kiami turned away from the window and reached out to pull herself onto Jacqueline's four-poster platform bed. Burying her face in its soft coverings, she breathed in deeply. The bedspread still smelled like her aunt.

Had she really unwittingly caused her own mother's death, as her aunt claimed? Neither Jacqueline nor Kiami's mother had seen malice in her eyes before. Her guardians had never questioned her intentions; instead, they focused on teaching her right from wrong. They told her never to be ashamed of who she was, believing that in time, with a strong set of moral values, Kiami would be able to use her abilities in some way to help the world.

It had cut her deeply when she saw the love drain from her aunt's eyes, replaced by the dull blackness of hatred. Perhaps if they hadn't been so attentive, Jacqueline's sudden change of heart wouldn't have startled her and hurt her so badly. Kiami knew her mother's illness and what happened on the beach were not connected. But the incident had helped to reinforce Jacqueline's theory that Kiami had somehow caused her mom's health to deteriorate. It was in her mind the only logical reason, not fate or gods or coincidence; someone had to be directly to blame. But it was no one's fault. It couldn't be.

And hadn't fate intervened well before Kiami came into their lives? Long before even Jacqueline had met her. The fact that her mother's name was Rhiannon was proof enough. A name that celebrated fertility bestowed upon a baby that would grow into an infertile woman.

And wasn't it fate and superstition that led them to each other and then to her? Jacqueline wasn't her biological aunt, but even so that was whom she had always been.

The loss of her mother and Jacqueline's ever-growing mistrust had devoured something inside of Kiami, and she wanted it back. She pulled the pillows tightly around her head and screamed into them. There was a muffled thump as something landed on the floor below her, and she lifted her head to peer over the side. A pale green cloth-bound book lay closed on the floor.

From her current position, it didn't appear that the book had any writing on the cover or spine.

She sat up and swung her legs over the side of the bed, sliding forward until her feet touched the floor. Then she bent to pick up the book, flipping it open to the first page. The name "Rhiannon" was written in the top left-hand corner in flowing cursive. Kiami touched the name lightly with her fingers and stepped forward to take Jacqueline's chair by the window. She looked up from the page as a wispy blue object darted out in front of her.

Her blood ran cold as she followed its movement. It stopped, hovering above the tea set next to another of the strange things. Kiami held her breath and dropped the book to the floor as she bolted for the bedroom door and through the hall. She stopped at the banister of the grand staircase and spun around as she breathed out.

The blue balls of light were only a few meters away and moving toward her. Kiami propelled herself up onto the banister, willing herself to change even as she moved. She jumped over the edge and glided down the two stories before maneuvering herself around the banister at the front of the staircase and back up the stairs, trying to remember if she had left the skylight open.

At just about sixty centimeters in length, it was much easier for Kiami to come in through the skylight than go out. She had to clutch the edge of the window frame with her talons and wiggle her owl body through the twenty-five-centimeter gap. She felt sharp, stinging sensations all over as several ruffled feathers tugged loose. Once on the roof, she made her way to the edge and dove over the side, gliding away from the house.

9

Kiami - The Owl and The Unicorn

Hitodama? If she was her humanoid self, she knew her arms and legs would be covered in goosebumps right now. *Human souls of the dead that have separated from their bodies.* Jacqueline and her mother had often told her lore about the world, and this one story in particular always frightened her. She circled the property several times before finally landing on the cliffs that stretched out over the ocean. Kiami shook out her feathers.

Was it possible that this specific bit of lore was true?

It was hard for Kiami to concentrate. The sound of the waves crashing against the shore was deafeningly loud when she was in owl form.

The pieces fit; she had been alone and filled with sorrow, and the blue orbs had found her. The souls she had left bodiless would haunt her home for all time.

Kiami sat down on the cool stone and pulled her knees to her chest. *I can't go back in there.* She cringed and looked down at her feet. A silver feather shimmered there, and she reached for it and ran her fingers over it. She had never found one of her own feathers before. A sudden gust of wind snatched it from her hand as it blew past her.

Kiami jumped up to chase after the feather, but the gust had only moved a short distance in front of her. The feather, as if caught in a tornado, swirled around more slowly with each rotation, and then it dropped to the ground next to a pair of shoes. Cautiously, Kiami moved her eyes over the figure.

Where did he come from?

"This is private property." She stood a full foot taller than the intruder. Dark hair hung around his face. Kiami smoothed out her white night dress. "You're welcome to enjoy the beach below. But up here is off limits."

Emerald-green eyes stared back at her. The stranger reached up and rubbed the back of his neck. "I'm sorry, I didn't mean to frighten you."

Kiami crossed her arms over her chest and glared at him. "There are much more frightening things in the world than you."

"Well, that is definitely true." He grinned and offered her his hand.

Kiami ignored the gesture and turned away from him, walking back toward the edge of the cliff.

"You're not thinking of jumping, are you?"

Kiami turned back and grimaced. "Please leave."

Had I been?

The realization that she could be forever unendingly alone here pulled at her. She wasn't even sure if she could die; her mother was given no manual and no warning of the things to come. The wispy blue creatures had frightened her, but there could be another explanation for them.

"I would like a heads-up so I can save you before you are swallowed up by the sea, that's all," he offered.

He's trying to be funny. She turned her eyes toward her home. She didn't want to stay here alone. The massive house hadn't seemed so utterly huge with her mom and aunt there with her.

"Kiami?"

She focused her eyes back on him and took a step back toward the cliff's jagged edge. "How do you know my name?"

"Whoa." Aden lifted his hands to his chest. "I'm not here to hurt you. I am here to tell you that you aren't alone. Could we maybe go inside and talk?"

Kiami held her hand out to signify that she didn't want him to come closer and shook her head before glancing down over the edge at the beach below. She didn't want to attract more people up to her home. Once she had him enthralled, she could send him on his way. The beach appeared to be deserted, and Kiami began to hum softly to herself, watching as he crossed his arms over his chest. She opened her mouth and started to sway to the sound as she let the song escape her lips.

She thought she saw a glimmer of something twinkle in his eye, and then he took an exaggerated step backward.

"Kiami, this is exactly what I wanted to talk to you about."

Kiami continued to move in time with the song, as if she hadn't heard him. She had never really thought about what she would do when she finally found someone that she couldn't enthrall, and she became giddy at the prospect.

With a sudden swift movement, she turned gracefully on her heel, bringing herself within inches of his forehead. She reached her arms up and wrapped them around him in a tight hug. Even in human form, her senses were much better than average, and she could hear his heartbeat echo in her ears. He didn't seem to be calm or relaxed.

Kiami released her grasp on him and stepped back. "Sorry. I got a little carried away."

I don't know anything about this guy.

"Yes, well, I'm Aden." He offered his hand again.

Kiami accepted, returning the loose shake. "I don't really want to go in there right now." She pointed in the direction of her house. *But I do want to know what else Aden knows about me.* "How did you know my name and where to find me?"

"That's something you will have to ask Amanda. She gave me your name and showed me where to find you on a map of this realm. She was fairly certain that you couldn't enthrall the jinn."

The words he was using were foreign. She searched her memory and came up empty. "Realm? the jinn? And who's Amanda?"

She watched as Aden reached up and rubbed the back of his neck before responding. "I'm a member of a race known as the jinn." He looked over his shoulder before responding again. "As I'm sure you know, magical beings like us are not commonplace in the Human realm, and I don't want to draw unwanted attention our way. We really should talk about this somewhere more private."

"Well, lead the way," Kiami said, extending her arm in an exaggerated motion.

Aden cocked his eyebrow. "You would go with me just like that?"

"I'm a big girl. I can handle myself." *Except when it comes to blue orbs of light.*

"Are you sure you're ready?"

"Are you trying to talk me out of it?"

"No, I..." Aden looked over his shoulder again, as if he was worried someone was watching. "Okay, just don't let go." He slid his arm around her waist, and Kiami felt the air kick up around her. The wind continued to swirl, encircling them as they moved. For Kiami, it was a familiar sensation, although she didn't feel free, like she did when she was soaring through the sky as an owl.

Then the wind suddenly changed direction, and for what only felt like a few seconds, they seemed to be nowhere, moving over a void. Kiami had to fight the urge to change form; she got the impression that Aden was unaware of her other abilities. *It may be best to keep it that way for now.*

Before long, her bare feet were once again firmly on the ground. Coarse grass brushed against her ankles. Kiami looked up into the night sky. This land somehow seemed both familiar and foreign. Stars sparkled and glistened above, while white silvery beams of unusually bright moonlight spilled down, illuminating the field.

"I thought we could walk from here."

Kiami threw him a half smile. *Is he stalling?*

"You're in the Arcane realm. I figured you might like to get familiar with the lay of the land around the castle. Besides, who doesn't like a moonlit stroll?" Aden bent his elbow and offered it to Kiami. She latched her arm through the opening and allowed him to lead her toward an inky pool of water in the distance. A pale band of silver stretched across the center of the pond. As they approached the water, Kiami could see faint ripples spreading outward from the other side.

Aden whispered, "Look closely." He pointed toward the middle of the pond. "Track the ripples to their point of origin." Kiami followed the ripples with her eyes to the water's edge where they began. A long snout poked down into the pond. The moonlight shone on the animal's sleek black hair. An equally dark mane unfurled from its head, around its ears, and down its muscular neck.

"A horse," Kiami whispered.

Aden released her arm. "Hardly. These animals only come out

at night. Look closer."

As if the horse-like creature had heard, it let out a snort and took a step into the pond's water. The moonbeam highlighted its head. Kiami gasped.

Taut hair covered the area on its face where she had expected large eyes to be located. A single spiral horn jutted from its forehead, jagged and sharp-looking. The animal snorted again and tossed its head back, causing its long mane to whip around.

"A unicorn?"

Aden shrugged and tugged at her arm. "We should go. Unicorns, as you call them, can seem pretty docile and innocent. Don't let the lack of eyes fool you; when they are hungry or annoyed, their prey doesn't stand a chance."

"Should we be worried?"

"Nah, he probably just smells something small, like a bird or rodent. They seem to use some kind of echolocation to hunt their prey, or maybe it's just magic. Don't worry, I wouldn't have shown you if I thought you were in any danger."

Kiami tightened her grip on his arm and picked up her pace, concentrating on smelling as human as possible. "So how far is the castle?"

"Just up ahead. You will hear it before you see it."

Kiami threw him another half-smile and glanced back in the direction they had come from. "Okay then."

She could see a crescent-shaped mountain ahead in the distance, and before long the sound of rushing water invaded her sensitive ears. As they drew closer, the noise increased steadily, and Kiami released Aden's arm as she took in the moonlit view.

Only a few hundred meters away, she was given a distorted glimpse of the castle. Sheets of water poured down from ledges that jutted out from somewhere up above, creating a glistening barrier that stretched the length of the ancient stone walls built within the mountainside. A single tower protruded up from the rectangular structure.

The water thundered in her sensitive ears as she drew closer. Fresh water sprayed at her, dampening her face and head. Kiami squinted, looking for a door, but could only make out a few windows, like great slits in the thick walls.

She turned to Aden and tried to shout above the noise. "How do we get inside?"

10

Amanda - Excitement and Jealousy

Amanda watched them from the slitted windows inside the walls of the castle. Her image of them was distorted by the water, which overflowed past the ledges that jutted outward from the mountain up above, spilling down around the fortification. A shiver of jealousy crept through her as she spied the blurred image of Aden wrapping his arm around Kiami's waist. She pursed her lips and folded her arms in front of her chest. She couldn't help but feel a little possessive of him. He had been her only friend since being ripped from the Human realm.

What reason do I have to be jealous? He's my companion, nothing else. She couldn't offer him anything deeper than that. Amanda felt broken, incapable of giving him more than her friendship, and he was pulling away, spending more and more time outside of the castle. The excitement she had felt about meeting Kiami crumbled and was replaced by resentment. What would Kiami's presence do to her friendship with Aden?

Fear, respect, and duty to the promise he had made were all that kept him coming back to her in this lonely place. Like her, he just had nowhere else to go, nowhere else he belonged. She thought of the strange village Emily had found. *Maybe he does have somewhere he could belong...* She squeezed her hand into a fist until she felt her nails dig into her skin. *Or it's a trap, and Emily wandered right in.* She needed to know more about Emily and what, exactly, her connection to this whole mess was.

She unclenched her fist and released a slow breath, keeping her eyes on the pair. It would only be a few moments before they were inside. She felt a new twinge of panic at their arrival. Realizing she was shrouded in darkness, Amanda whispered an incantation as she struck a match and reached up to light one of the sconces that lined the walls.

She stood on her toes and blew softly into the flame, causing it to jump up as if it had come to life. It made its way from one sconce to the next, all the way around the room, lighting each as it landed.

Everything in the castle seemed to have been spelled by the sorcerer in one way or another, and Amanda had learned a great many of his parlor tricks from the books he kept in the library.

They were just that, tricks. Her real power came from the very thing that made her uneasy: the shadows. Just because she could make the shadows move for her didn't mean she liked the dark. She found it suffocating and lonely.

As the room brightened, so did her mood, and a smile spread across her face.

"I can do this."

A sudden rush of wind caressed Amanda's skin and blew through her hair. The candle flames flickered wildly as a whirling mass of air appeared and then disappeared almost as quickly, leaving in its path Aden and Kiami.

Amanda cleared her throat and ran her fingers through her wind-swept tresses as she studied Kiami's tall, willowy figure. Her almond-shaped eyes shimmered a strange metallic silver above her high, delicate cheekbones.

She had not fathomed the sheer intensity of Kiami's unique beauty. This was a girl that guys would trip over themselves to help. Which explained why, even without the aid of Kiami's song, the boy on the beach had welcomed the stranger into his arms. She wondered what Jacqueline's cryptic message had meant; she saw no resemblances to herself in her visitor.

"You must be Kiami." Amanda extended her arm to her guest. Kiami accepted it, yanking Amanda forward into a hug. Caught off guard by the sudden embrace, Amanda hesitated before she reached up with her free hand and gave Kiami's shoulder a quick pat. She took an awkward step backward.

Amanda wasn't used to this type of physical affection from a stranger. Not sure how to react to her guest's greeting, she spun around to face Aden. "You returned much sooner than I expected."

Aden's smile melted as his gazed shifted from Kiami to Amanda and then down at his feet. "She was in a hurry to meet you." He took a cautious step back, stumbling slightly. Amanda let out an uneasy giggle and glanced back at her guest.

Kiami had a blank expression; her eyes were fixed on the ragged scars that ran across Amanda's bare shoulders.

Amanda crossed her arms in front of her chest. "And I am thrilled to finally meet her, but..." She turned away from them and stared back out of the slitted window at the moon. "You both must be very tired. Maybe it would be best to talk in the morning. It's late."

Aden's footsteps echoed in the quiet room as he approached her and grabbed her arm. "Are you feeling all right?"

"Yes, I just need some sleep. Why don't you show our guest to a bedroom where she can get some rest?"

"As you wish."

Amanda turned back as they moved hand in hand through the doorway and out into the hall. She followed behind slowly and then turned left as they turned right through the passageway.

Kiami's whisper carried through the corridor to her ears. "Did I do something wrong?" It brought Amanda to a stop outside the bedroom she now claimed as her own.

"No, she's just ... Amanda, I mean she's been through a lot. Don't take offense."

"I thought you said she sent you to get me. She acts like she hates me already."

"Come on, I will give you a quick tour of the castle before you settle in for the night. Maybe I can answer some of your questions along the way."

Amanda leaned against the door frame, listening for another moment as the sound of their footsteps faded away.

Amanda wasn't content as she lay on her bed. Used to falling asleep in the library, she would overwork her brain until she could no longer form a coherent thought.

The stiff mattress felt unfamiliar. She tossed and turned, trying to get comfortable. The coarse blanket scratched at her bare skin.

Amanda kicked it to the floor, folded her hands over her stomach, and stared up at the ceiling, waiting for her heavy eyelids to give in.

The whispers were barely audible at first. Confused, Amanda strained to hear, expecting Aden and Kiami's voices...

"He's going to leave you here all alone," the creature breathed. The gravelly sound scratched at her ears. Frazzled by Kiami, she had forgotten all about her nighttime tormentor. She still only thought of him as a grinning monster that invaded her mind while she slept, although she had recently learned that the jinn called him Abaddon.

"How long did you think he would remain content to stay in this gloomy castle with someone as frigid as you? And you led him right to her..."

Amanda commanded her muscles to move, but it was no use. Her body was in a deep state of sleep, but her mind was wide awake. She tried to close herself back off, but once she had opened herself up completely to him, she was unable to recreate a barricade.

"Since the day at the tomb, he has grown more and more distant." His words stung. "You're a beauty, Amanda, but not like her, because you are rotten inside."

Amanda's eyes shot open involuntarily. His grin was wider than that of a normal man. His mouth gaped open from ear to ear, his rotten yellow teeth ending in unnaturally sharp points. "I'm going to tell you a secret, Amanda." The air from his breath whistled through his misshapen teeth as he breathed out, "That village you're planning on sending them to is full of jinn like Jacqueline. Think about what you're doing, Amanda."

She sat up suddenly, gasping. Beads of sweat rolled off her skin. The droplets ran down her face and limbs. Was her search for information about Emily worth the possibility of losing Aden's friendship? She pulled her knees up to her chest and counted slowly to herself as she breathed in and out. Could it be possible that Abaddon was lying? She didn't know what motivated him; she only knew that his warning made sense. *Hadn't I had a similar fear all along?* During the vision of Emily, she had sensed something was off; she just hadn't been able to put her finger on what it was.

The sun had barely risen. The first orange-hued rays that should have brought warmth to a new day only acted to solidify the reality that her time was running out. Every time she learned something new, more questions grew from the answers. *How did an entire village of jinn end up in the Human realm, and why were they so quick to offer help to Emily?*

Amanda wished that the sun would sink back down below the horizon so she could have more time to process, but you can't argue with the sun.

11

Amanda - Jinn and Spies

Until Amanda reached the open door to the library, she had seen no sign of Aden or her guest. She peeked around the side of the entrance.

Kiami stood in front of a row of cluttered shelves, studying the spines of the unorganized books.

Amanda spoke quickly as she stepped into the room. "You will find that most of those are not written in any human language."

Kiami turned her head to peer over her shoulder. "I didn't mean to invade your space." She backed up away from the shelving and turned to Amanda. "Aden mentioned that you spend most of your time in here, so I figured you would show up eventually."

Amanda crossed her arms in front of her chest and raised one of her eyebrows. "And where is Aden?"

Kiami shrugged. "He went out." A frown settled on her face as she took a tentative step toward Amanda. "Last night, he told me a bit about how you both ended up here. I, I didn't mean to stare, I have just never seen such..."

Amanda raised a hand to shush her. "That's enough, it's fine. I'm relieved that he filled you in." She plastered a smile on her face. "I assume he explained somewhat about the realms, then, and why I asked him to bring you. I mean, you traveled here, so he must have said something..."

Kiami shuffled her feet and cleared her throat. "I am more than a little curious ... but I guess ... I'm a little embarrassed to say, I was in a hurry to get away from my home."

Amanda curled her lip. "Was it really so lonely in your mansion by the sea that you would take off with a complete stranger?" She reached forward and patted Kiami's hand lightly.

Kiami didn't flinch. "You are being kind of rude, for someone that sought me out for help."

"Well, maybe so. I admit I am in a terrible mood. I haven't had a good night's sleep in a long time. I would like you to help me with that." Amanda's smile grew as she spoke. "I hoped for you the mission would be a welcome distraction, given your recent experiences. I know how it feels to be torn from the things you know, your reality shifting in such a way that you feel lost and desperate..."

Kiami fidgeted again, visibly unsettled. "How do you even know anything about me?"

Amanda rolled her eyes. "Relax, I want us to be friends ... but you need to tell me the truth."

"There was something in my house, spirits, blue balls of wispy smoke. They were following me."

"Wisps?" Amanda forced out an unnecessary giggle.

"Honestly," Kiami folded her arms in front of her, "how does Aden put up with you?"

"I'm sorry." Amanda shrugged. "It's just I don't think they meant you harm. When I was being held here, blue wisp creatures, like the ones you described, saved my life..." She reached out and ran her fingers over the shelf of books in front of her as if checking for dust.

"I am a bit curious, though. You said you thought they were after you. Why?" Amanda reached for Kiami's hand and grasped it. "Are you evil, Kiami? Do you feel like you are an abomination?"

Kiami looked away. "We all have demons."

"Oh honey, you have no idea. But you will. I think we have a lot of catching up to do..." Amanda looked around thoughtfully. "And I guess this is as good a place as any." She lowered herself down onto the stone floor with her legs crisscrossed beneath her and observed Kiami as she spoke.

"It's disappointing, isn't it? From the outside there's an enchanting scene. It looks magical, like something from a fairy tale, the vast field, a shimmering pond, the waterfalls spraying down. But once you're inside, it's just a damp, gloomy castle." Amanda wrinkled her nose. "Magic isn't pretty at all ... but I think you already know something about that."

Kiami gracefully knelt down onto the hard floor across from her and cocked her head to the side. "You're not a prisoner anymore. If you're unhappy here, why don't you just leave?" Curiosity danced in her eyes.

Amanda looked down at her hands. "That's what I thought too, but then I..." She drew in a deep breath and looked back up at Kiami. "We are getting off topic." She pushed herself back up off the floor. "The world we grew up in obviously isn't all there is. As you can see."

She moved to one of the overflowing shelves as she continued. "Basic world mythology 101, condensed version." She turned back to Kiami and winked before continuing. "Legend claims that the magical races and humans once lived together, but that after humans were nearly wiped out, the other humanoid beings were divided by race and separated into these realms to stop them from waging war against each other." Amanda pulled a small worn book from one of the shelves and made her way back toward Kiami. "You see, humans don't have natural magic, or at least that's what the stories claim."

Kiami cocked her head. "This veil thing that separates the realms, how did we travel through it, if it's meant to keep us away from one another?"

Amanda handed the delicate book over to Kiami. "A jinni once told me that magic is not meant to be understood, and I admit that much of jinn culture is still a mystery to me. Aden being taken so young, his knowledge is limited..."

Amanda lowered herself back to the floor. "The jinn seem to have an easier time traveling from realm to realm in general. In order for me to accompany Aden to the Emerald Mountains, where he had lived before he was taken by Jacob, additional magic was needed. Strong magic." Amanda took another deep breath before continuing. "The exact hows and whys are something we could debate for hours. It's probably best that we stick with the essentials for now. In that notebook, there is some information on the jinn you may find useful for your journey."

Kiami sat up a little taller and cleared her throat before she opened her mouth. "You mean *if* I decide to go, and aren't you two coming with me?"

"Aden can return you to the Human realm and take you to a place nearby, but there's much more to it than he knows, you see." Amanda lowered her voice to a whisper and leaned in closer to Kiami. "Aden is like a brother to me, and I'm trying to protect him. What did he tell you about where he comes from, his people?"

Kiami furrowed her brow. "Well, he really didn't say much about himself or the jinn at all."

Amanda nodded. She had been counting on the fact that he would leave out certain painful memories, and she would be able to embellish them. "That's what I thought." She sat back up. "You see, when we went to his home realm, his village had been abandoned. His reaction to the empty huts was, well ... it was hard to bear witness to. We could have traveled over the mountain range that encircled that valley to look for other jinn clans, but he wanted to forget them just as he had been forgotten.

"As for me, as eager as I am to know why there is a jinn village in the Human realm and what they are hiding, I believe they would not tolerate my presence. Aden told you that even as I suffered at the hands of Jacob, I learned that magic is in my blood?"

Kiami nodded.

"It seems I am a descendant of the enemies of the jinn, and so it's my belief that they will not openly accept me, much less tolerate my presence for long. You at least have a chance where I have none."

"How do you know they will accept me?"

"I guess I don't, but I am fairly certain that your natural magic doesn't come from the same place as mine." *What had Bloise said about the song magic that had enthralled her all that time ago?* She couldn't quite remember. Amanda pushed the thought away. It was a question for another time, but the old wizard could definitely be useful.

"Kiami, I want you to lay low at first, play it by ear. There's a girl there, Emily ... she is not a jinni, and yet they seem to want to protect her. And if you can manage it, I want you to find out why. You need to be careful. Jinni can have a plethora of abilities, and your song doesn't affect them."

"Yes, how did you know about that?"

Amanda avoided the direct question. "It's why I believe I can help you. I have seen the way you can control those around you with your song, and I have seen it before ... in a palace, run by a wizard name Bloise ... and if you want to explore that further, we will. *After* you are done with your mission."

Kiami gave a slight nod but didn't seem a bit surprised at the offer, so Amanda continued.

"When Aden still lived in the Emerald Mountains with the jinn, he was taught that a jinni takes on traits as they mature and that these traits are decided by the choices the jinni make." Amanda leaned forward and patted Kiami's hand. "You should know," a sly smile crept over her face, "jinn mature very slowly. Even as a youngling, Aden was already decades older than any human." She paused, hoping for a reaction, but Kiami's smile didn't waver and her eyes remained locked in a thoughtful stare even as Amanda watched Aden walk into the room.

Amanda hopped to her feet. "The jinn are rather mischievous. One trait they all seem to have is that they can choose to be seen or unseen, if they wish, and it appears that you, wherever you come from, unlike me, are not immune to this."

"Are you saying Aden is here now?"

"He's only just arrived." Amanda reached her arm out and wrapped it around Aden's invisible shoulder as he shimmered into view.

12

Kiami - Black Diamond

Kiami waited on the wall walk, high above the ground, breathing in the fresh outside air. She had only been a guest here for a few days, and already she felt a bit restless. All her life, her mother and Jacqueline had been preparing her to meet people like herself by telling her myths and legends from all over the world.

She had racked her brain, poring over those memories all night, and she was quite sure that none of the stories told had ever mentioned the race of jinn or anything about the separation of the realms, and it didn't surprise her. They simply hadn't known which stories were true and which had been conjured up by overactive imaginations. Only humans themselves, they had done their best.

Kiami leaned over the edge and peered down, wishing she could go ahead without Amanda and Aden, but she was still reluctant to let on that she had the ability to transform into an owl, and if they found her waiting on the ground below, she would have to reveal her secret.

It had been Aden's suggestion that had prompted this foray into the Arcane realm; he felt that they could learn something from each other's abilities. Amanda had readily agreed to a demonstration, and Kiami had gotten the impression from her that she had wanted to show her she wasn't someone to mess with.

Kiami wanted to tell her that her tough girl act wasn't necessary. She wouldn't have even needed to offer up a meeting with Bloise as compensation. She wanted to know more about Amanda, and even with the possibility of danger, the idea of being in a town filled with magical beings fascinated her.

As the pair emerged, it was obvious they had been arguing. Amanda's cheeks were crimson, her arms were folded in front of her, and the look she was giving Aden could have frightened a few feathers right off Kiami if she wasn't in human form.

"Why do we have to do this down there?" Her voice was demanding as she spoke to Aden, and Kiami wondered how she could prove to Amanda that she was not a threat, but she supposed only time would accomplish that.

"I already explained this to you, Amanda." Unlike when they first arrived, Aden's voice didn't falter as he pleaded his case. "For one, your magic is stronger in the shadows. For another thing, you don't have good control of it, especially when you combine your power with the gem. You could end up bringing the castle down on us."

Kiami tried not to eavesdrop as Aden lowered his voice to a whisper and reached for Amanda's arm. "Besides, the fresh air will do you some good. I can hardly remember the last time I saw you outside."

A look of worry had settled on Amanda's face, but she gave a curt nod to Aden before glancing upward to meet Kiami's gaze.

Compelled to add something to the conversation, Kiami blurted, "It took me years to gain good control over my song. When I was a young girl I..." She saw Amanda roll her eyes and look away. *I think I just made it worse.* Kiami bit her tongue and threw an apologetic look at Aden.

"Kiami, I will take Amanda down first then come back for you."

"You're going to leave me down there?" Kiami thought she heard a hint of fear in Amanda's voice. It was obvious that painful memories remained, and she wanted to avoid them. Kiami could understand that, but she couldn't comprehend why Amanda wouldn't just come out and say it now, like when she had told Kiami why she avoided the Human realm.

"It's just for a minute. Taking both of you at once is something I would only do if I had to."

"Fine." Kiami watched as Amanda placed her arm around his waist. "Just hurry up."

A moment later, when he returned, he offered Kiami only a shrug as explanation before he told her to grab on to him for her own descent from the castle wall.

Even though clouds blocked the majority of the midday sun that lingered overhead, Kiami was happy to be out in the pure air without the cold stones of the castle floors underfoot.

Aden was on her heels as she followed close behind Amanda. She seemed distracted, glancing around frequently as she plowed ahead through grass and weeds.

They had only been walking a few minutes when Amanda stopped and peered over her shoulder. "So Aden, what's the plan? Surely you don't want me to focus my magic on you or Kiami."

Kiami spun around to face the direction they had come from and was disappointed to see that they had only moved a few yards from the castle. She had been looking forward to exploring more of the Arcane realm.

"No, of course not," Aden said, and Kiami watched as he turned in a circle. "Over there, focus on cracking that big rock."

Water pooled around the boulder he was referring to, causing it to resemble a small-scale replica of an island. A few tiny flower buds sprouted up from the green and brown moss that covered a great deal of the rock's surface, adding to the effect. The water that had formed around it, Kiami presumed, was excess runoff from the falls.

Three small, twisted horns popped up from the backside of the boulder, followed by two big, round eyes. Kiami cocked her head at the strange-looking lizard and was surprised to see it mirror her movement. A coincidence, she thought.

She knew that her companions wouldn't be able to pick out the same fine details of the boulder and its occupant from this distance, and she doubted that a lizard would have better sight than her own.

She was still studying the creature when she heard a faint static sound fill the air around her. Was this what Amanda's magic felt like? The hair on her arms and neck prickled, and she turned to see what Amanda was doing.

She stood just a few feet away. Several shadows seemed to extend along the ground at Amanda's feet, regardless of the presence of daylight. One of her hands was held out in front of her as she stared in the direction of the boulder. The hand seemed to be wrapped tightly around something; Kiami assumed it was the black diamond they had mentioned before.

Transfixed by the scene, Kiami had almost forgotten the lizard creature. It wasn't until Amanda shouted, "Watch out!" that she remembered the little animal, and she was helpless to do anything for it as a wave of magic shot out from Amanda, headed straight at the boulder. The ground below them groaned and rumbled as it ripped the grass and flowers up along its path.

The rock didn't just crack with the impact; it exploded, shooting pieces through the air in all directions. Kiami let out a gasp as she moved to inspect the empty crater where the boulder had been.

She didn't notice anything extraordinary about the appearance of the bowl-shaped cavity when she looked into it. If she hadn't witnessed the exploding boulder first-hand, she would never have thought twice about it.

Kiami had expected Amanda and Aden to join her at the site of impact. Realizing they hadn't joined her, she called out to them, "So is this what always happens?"

Amanda looked up and shrugged. "I really have only used shadow magic a few times. I guess Aden's right; I need to learn to control it better."

Kiami moved toward the pair as Amanda looked back down at Aden. He had lowered himself onto all fours and was inspecting something in the grass. "What kind of lizard is that?"

"I haven't ever seen one in this realm before," Aden answered just as Kiami stepped up beside him. He hovered above the horned lizard she had seen just before Amanda let her magic loose. This creature wasn't scaled; instead, its skin looked smooth and even. Lying still in the grass, the creature looked to be six or seven inches long. Each of its four appendages ended in three long, suction-cupped fingers.

Surprised at Amanda's silence, Kiami asked, "What do you mean 'in this realm' Aden?"

"Forget it, I must be mistaken. Unless... It's just that it bears a striking resemblance to a symbiotic bloodsucking creature I once found." He leaned back on his heels and looked up at Kiami and Amanda. "In its native realm, the people referred to it as a grindyliz, and many kept them as companions, kind of like a pet. They are very intelligent, you see, and they never latch on before making friends. Or at least that's what I was told."

Kiami's curiosity about this other realm was piqued; she wanted to know more about where this creature might have come from. Aden looked up into her eyes, and she hung on his words. "You see, the realm they live in is cold. Snow covers the ground almost all the time, so the beings they bond with also share their warmth."

Amanda let out an exaggerated sigh, interrupting their chatter. "All that is most interesting, Aden, but animals can't jump from realm to realm any more easily than the rest of us, so obviously you are dealing with something else entirely here." She pointed down at the small creature, and Kiami looked away, disturbed by her indifferent behavior.

Aden spoke up, still addressing Kiami. "Maybe we should bury the little guy."

Kiami looked back at him and shook her head. "Yes, let's do that."

After this was all over, she would look forward to visiting the other realms. But first she needed to learn more about herself. The other realms and how exactly she could travel between them without Aden was a mystery to her — one she hoped to unravel as she conducted Amanda's mission.

13

Emily - Weeds

A dandelion peeked out from a crack in the sidewalk. Emily hadn't noticed it yesterday when she had stood in this very spot. *Do they always grow that fast? And under such harsh conditions?* It may have been a weed, but she thought its yellow hue was beautiful. Stooping for a better examination, she could see no apparent flaws at all. Its only crime was to be a simple weed. The idea that it had managed to push itself through layers of earth, rock, and cement with such a seemingly dainty stem perplexed her. Abandoning the weed to its hopeless situation, she returned to her post inside the shop, saddened by the fact that it was inevitable that the dandelion would be plucked or chopped or crushed in the near future after managing to persevere through its struggle to the surface in such unfriendly territory.

I'm not supposed to be here either, Emily thought. Taking her place back behind the register, she pulled her purple-streaked hair up and into a messy ponytail.

"Good break?" Gemma called from behind the swinging half door that separated the front of the pet boutique from the grooming area.

This job had been hers for the last three months. And it was all thanks to Gemma that she had managed to last here in town as long as she had. Gemma worried after her in a way her own mother hadn't since she had discovered her gift.

"Mmhmm," she responded, distracted by memories of a time before she had changed.

Reaching into her pocket, she touched the palm-sized crystal. The purple jewel was a memento from her past. It was always within reach. It made her feel calmer, just as Gemma's mothering did.

The bell jingled above the door, and Emily greeted the sharp-nosed Mrs. Nazari and her poodle, Ori.

"Hello, Zia," Gemma called out. "I will be right with you." Emily could feel Mrs. Nazari's eyes looking her up and down. Her lips were set in a tight line on her wrinkled face. *What did I ever do to her?*

"Em, why don't you go take an early lunch? Bring me back something."

Emily didn't bother to argue the fact that she had only just returned from a break and took her leave quickly, glad to be away from the scrutinizing glare of Mrs. Nazari.

Emily walked slowly, letting her mind wander. She often

felt the strange sensation that she was being watched, but she chalked it up to past bad experiences and did her best to seem at ease, fighting the urge to look back over her shoulder.

This quaint town was different somehow. The way Gemma had offered her a job the moment she had stepped into her shop, removing the "Help Wanted" sign before she ever had a chance to utter a reply. Emily had come to appreciate the way the members of the community always greeted her by name when she walked into their small businesses, not getting up to follow her around as if she was a suspect in an inevitable heist. With the exception of Mrs. Zia Nazari, everyone smiled at her warmly, as if they had known her for ages.

Emily knew it would be the hardest move she would ever have to make when she had to leave this place. A car honked, and she looked up, half expecting to see the driver shaking his fist in the air and muttering, but was met instead by the calm light-green eyes that were so predominant in town. Emily waved at the smiling driver as she moved out of the way. This time, she looked for more cars before attempting to move across the street.

As she approached One Last Bite, a familiar face smiled at her through the large glass windows. It seemed to Emily that

Cherry never had a day off. She couldn't remember ever walking through the restaurant's doors and not seeing her taking orders or chatting with patrons.

One Last Bite had become her go to eatery for lunch. Its red-and-white awning stood out amid the dull gray-and-green patterns of the surrounding businesses. Once inside, it became even clearer that this business was unique; the stark white walls and clean appearance gave her a feeling of newness that couldn't be found in another building she had ventured into. The fact that it was different was what brought her back day after day. Like her, the restaurant stuck out amidst the town like a sore thumb.

Emily slid onto the soft red vinyl seat of an empty booth and breathed in deeply. The scent of freshly baked pastries invaded her nose as she pulled her current paperback novel from her purse and placed it on the shiny chrome surface of the tabletop.

"You're here a bit earlier than usual today. What can I get for you?" Cherry grinned down at her, holding her pen and pad at attention. "Would you like to hear the specials?"

"No, thanks. Just a cola and a turkey sandwich, and can you wrap an order of the house soup to go, please?"

"No pie, then?" Cherry glanced up at Emily while she scribbled, adding, "It *is* our specialty."

"Not right now, thanks."

"Okay, I'll have that drink right out to you." Cherry whistled as she strolled away to put in the order, her ponytail swaying from side to side the same way her hips did.

Emily picked up her book, a mystery she'd got for a quarter at the used bookstore down the street. She enjoyed visiting the dusty shop and sorting through the stacks of books that lined the walls. At first she had been discouraged that none of the books seemed to be in any type of recognizable order, but after a few visits, sorting through them had become a game, and more often than not, she would end up leaving with a stack of them.

She wasn't really enjoying this particular book all that much, but it made her look busy, something Emily had decided was important here. If you looked busy, people were less apt to stop and make small talk, less apt to ask questions about her, questions she didn't want to answer.

Her ploy to be left undisturbed during her lunch didn't last long. Within minutes her drink arrived, right along with her sandwich, and someone slid onto the seat in front of her. For a second, she thought Gemma had decided to join her.

Emily looked over the top of her book and rolled her eyes. Justin's grin seemed to stretch from ear to ear.

"You still ignoring me, Emily?"

"Ignoring you?" she asked, but she knew what he meant. Although her aloofness wasn't aimed at him alone, as a rule she didn't go out of her way to start conversations with anyone in town. But ever since her first encounter with the young man, she tended to take the long route around if she thought there would be any possibility of bumping into him.

"Well then, mind if I join you?"

"Gemma will be coming..." The lie caught in her throat as Cherry sat a to-go bag on the table beside her plate.

"Here's Gemma's lunch." Cherry placed her hand on her hip. "You sure she wouldn't like some pie?"

Emily sank lower into her seat and rested her eyes back on the open pages of her book, "Pumpkin is her favorite, I think," she murmured just loud enough to be heard. *Does Cherry know she just blew my cover?*

"Sounds right, coming up!" Cherry added as she hurried off.

Ugh. Emily released a sigh and dropped her book back onto the table. "Are you going to order something, or did you just come in to bother me?"

Justin looked thoughtful as he ran his hand through his wavy, dark hair. "I think I will have some house soup." He turned in his seat and casually laid his arm over the backrest. "Yo, Cherry," he bellowed. "Bring me some of that great soup and a water, please."

"Nice." *What is with this guy?* Emily thought as she rolled her eyes again. "You know, she would have come back in a minute," she added, picking at the lettuce on her sandwich.

Justin turned back toward her and rested his arms on the table. "Oh, Cherry loves me, she doesn't mind..." He leaned forward as if he was about to add something but pushed himself back into an upright position just as another to-go bag suddenly appeared on the table between them.

The seasoned waitress juggled a large tray on one arm as she placed the soup and a water in front of Justin. She turned to Emily. "Are you sure you don't want anything else to eat?" She eyed Emily up and down with a playful smirk. "You're practically skin and bones."

Emily pushed her plate away. "No, thanks, I am pretty full. Could I have the check please?"

Justin cleared his throat and winked at Emily before addressing Cherry. "Add it to mine. It's the least I can do after spoiling her lunch."

Emily took another swallow from her glass. "Do you have something in your eye?"

He leaned forward again, and Emily moved to stuff her book back into her purse. "I better get back to work. Thanks for the sandwich."

Justin nodded, once again sitting back. "No rest for the wicked, right?" He grinned at her as she stood and moved away from the table, pausing only momentarily to return a wave to Cherry before hurrying out the door.

The hairs on Emily's neck prickled as the door swung lightly shut behind her. She glanced toward the window near her booth. Justin stared back out at her. Emily moved to the street's edge and looked both ways before glancing back over her shoulder again. Now Justin appeared to be leaning over his bowl, concentrating on his soup.

Still, the uneasy feeling remained, as if someone's eyes were burrowing into her. Emily glanced around suspiciously. Instead of crossing the street, she continued down the road away from Gemma's shop. She stopped in front of the heavy oak door of the five and dime. There was only one small display window in front, and it was always completely covered with fliers. Emily stood there a moment and took a deep breath before pushing the door open. Once inside, she leaned back against the door and rubbed the goosebumps on her arms.

Mr. Asad let out a chuckle from his seat by the register. "Hiding from someone, Emily?"

Emily raised her hand to her chest, startled. "No, sorry, just got..."

He pulled his glasses forward to the tip of his nose and looked out at her from above the frames. "The heebie jeebies, like someone was watchin ya?" He furrowed his already wrinkly brow and set down the papers he had been looking through.

Did he always have an accent? Maybe I didn't hear him correctly. Emily raised an eyebrow as she took a few steps toward the register, studying the youthful blue eyes that looked back at her, as if they hadn't aged with the rest of him. "A chill. I forgot my jacket."

"Uh-huh-uh-huh." He nodded. "S'pose ta get downright cold by tomara."

Maybe there's something wrong with me? Emily wrinkled her brow and fumbled with one of the small bags that were placed out on the counter for what Mr. Asad referred to as dime-store candy. *What day is it? It's soon...* She perused the glass display jars to find the red licorice. *Might as well not leave empty-handed.*

Mr. Asad picked his papers back up and shuffled them. "It's always the third one on tha left, Em." He smiled up at her from his work. "And it's on the house taday,"

"Um, thanks," she stammered. *Is it me or is everyone acting weird today?* No one besides Gemma had ever called her Em before. *Not here, anyway.* Since when didn't she have to pay her own way? *It's just a weird coincidence,* she assured herself. *Better safe than sorry.*

"Will there be anything else you need taday?"

"Could I use your bathroom? I know the shop is right across the street but..."

"Of course, dear," he said before she could finish her sentence. "In back and down tha hall."

"Thanks," she muttered as she weaved through the disorganized racks and aisles of household items toward the back of the store.

Safely inside the small bathroom, she looked at herself in the mirror. The same eyes stared back at her; nothing had changed. She let down her raven hair, combing through it with her fingers, causing the tight curls to spring back. The seemingly unnatural purple strands moved in unison with the rest. *At least normal for me, anyway.* Emily squinted at her reflection, trying to remember what she had looked like before her eleventh birthday.

To Emily, her appearance had almost seemed to change overnight. It wasn't until she returned to school that she realized how cruel people could be. She hadn't known how to explain the strange changes to her classmates without talking about what she had done to the bird. At first she had insisted to them that her hair had grown in naturally, and they laughed at her.

Only Vanessa had tried to believe her without question. She even tried to help Emily recolor her hair, but no matter what shade they chose, the purple always shone through. Her friend didn't give up, though. Together they experimented with beauty products, attempting to make her eyes once again appear the hazel everyone was used to. They found that with the right application of eyeshadows and liners, Emily could mask the purple flecks that now dotted her irises, causing her eye color almost to seem like a deep brown.

Emily opened her eyes wider and turned her head from side to side. She hadn't so much as donned a pair of sunglasses to hide her eye color since leaving home, and no one here had seemed to notice.

Satisfied she hadn't sprouted horns, Emily walked up to the front of the store, gave a wave, and headed back to Gemma's pet boutique.

As she opened the door to resume her post for Gemma, the realization that she had left her food order behind dawned on her. She stomped the heel of her boot down. "Shoot." Justin had her all distracted.

"There you are. We were getting worried." Gemma said. "Justin here was nice enough to bring my lunch over." She gestured to Justin, who was leaning on the counter.

He looked up at her and grinned. "I told Gemma you had pressing business at the five and dime."

It was him that was watching me. Emily felt her face grow hot. "Sorry, I just needed to go grab something. I'm not late..."

"No, you're not," Gemma reassured her. "Are you feeling okay? You look a little green."

"No, yes, I'm fine." Her stomach was turning all of a sudden. But she had to pay for her bed and eat. The room where she lived wasn't much, but it was shelter. At least she could come and go as she needed. She shuddered at the memory of the phantom lifestyle she had endured before she had wandered into town. She may have been locked in her room, but she had never felt safe. Not that she felt completely safe, even here in this town. *It is only a matter of time.* Her hand slipped into her pocket. She was thinking of the amethyst there, wondering, *Is it possible someone saw it?* Maybe they had, and they had told others. They would certainly want to take the stone from her.

"Emily, did you hear me?" Gemma asked, snapping her fingers in front of Emily's face. "Earth to Emily."

"What, sorry, maybe I'm just a little tired." Lost in her own thoughts, she had not been listening to Gemma and Justin.

"Justin here was just saying how nice it will be when the two of you go into the neighboring village for dinner tonight."

"What?" Emily gasped as Justin made a swift movement

toward the door.

He grabbed the handle and yanked the door open. "Pick you up here at five, Emily."

As the door shut behind him, Emily turned back to Gemma. "He never asked me on a date."

"Emily, you were probably not paying attention, just like a moment ago. If you haven't noticed, when you're not working on something, you are not the most focused person." She placed a hand on Emily's shoulder. "You drift off somewhere."

"Sorry," Emily said sheepishly.

"Oh, Emily, don't be, it's just you. You're a great worker and a good person. Maybe a little shy at times, or most of the time." Gemma shrugged. "Just don't worry about it. Go have fun. Young girls do that, you know."

Emily chewed at her bottom lip. "I have fun."

"Oh?" Gemma raised her eyebrows.

"Okay, okay. I will go." Emily grinned. "Stop being such a mom."

"Hmm, I don't think so. Besides, you know that's what you like about me, Emily."

"Maybe," she said. *More than you know.*

Gemma pulled out her inventory books from beneath the counter. "Why don't you go start cleaning up in the back? We don't have any more appointments today."

Emily raised her hand in a salute and marched to the back of the shop to sweep and sanitize.

Her thoughts returned to Justin as she worked. There weren't many teenagers in town for her to get to know, and she wondered if she had been avoiding a conversation with him more than anyone else. Her face grew warm as she used the broom to move a pile of debris onto the dustpan and into the garbage pail.

He had been the second person she had come into contact with after arriving in town months ago, and it hadn't been the most pleasant encounter for her.

Paranoia had hit as soon as she exited Gemma's shop. With the envelope for Nina clutched in her hand, she darted back across the street to the center of town. She stared down at her hand. The whole encounter had seemed so surreal. Emily felt like she was in a dream.

Gemma had instructed her to cross the town square and continue through to the other side of the street. Emily chewed at her lip, wondering if she should turn around and return the envelope. It seemed to her that bad things had followed her since she left home.

What if I accept her help and end up causing her harm like that poor little boy, Toby? Gemma had seemed sincere enough about wanting to help, but so had Bav. What if she ended up being like her?

She scolded herself. *You're not going to get anywhere if you're not willing to take some chances. You might as well still be with your parents, locked in your room every night.*

A shiver ran up her spine as she spun toward the tree that sat in the center of the square. She had sworn that she saw movement from within its branches. She dropped her arm to her side and peered up at the strange, tree-shaped carving. The hair on the back of her neck prickled; she felt like someone was watching her. *Stone trees don't move, and they certainly don't watch you. You're being ridiculous.*

Emily forced herself to take steady steps past the tree and across to the other side of the street. She hoped the creeping feeling would fade as she got farther away. Gemma had instructed her to turn right and walk along the sidewalk until she came to a small paved road.

Soon she arrived at a gap in the row of stores. The opening didn't look quite wide enough for two vehicles to pass through at the same time, but the only other visible road was the one that wrapped around the town square, allowing access to the loop of businesses. Emily had never seen a town that only had one road in and out, it did explain why Gemma's instructions had merely been to follow the road to the residential area.

Another shiver ran up her spine. She couldn't seem to shake the idea that someone was watching her. She turned the corner and leaned against the wall before peeking back out. No one was visible along the main street in either direction.

Disappointed, she turned back. At least if someone had been there, she would have had a reason for feeling like eyes were boring holes into her. Emily wrung her hands as she walked beyond the shadow of the buildings. She could see that the pavement continued toward a spattering of houses in the distance. A fast crunch on the gravel behind her caused her to jerk her head back around.

No one was visible along the path. Emily was suddenly aware that she could feel her heart thumping in her chest. She spun her head back toward the homes just as another crunch noise filled her ears.

Gemma had told her to look for a house with bright pink shutters; she had even mentioned that the door should be unlocked. She squinted, trying to pinpoint its location, and took off jogging toward it. By the time she reached the front steps, she was shaky and out of breath.

Still on edge, instead of stopping to knock, she had flung open the door and collided head on with Justin. Even after the shock of the collision, she pushed past him, slamming the door behind her.

She had been so upset that when a woman had appeared from around the corner, she hadn't even been able to form a full coherent sentence and just thrust the note from Gemma out at her.

When she finally calmed down, she learned that she had given Justin a bloody lip.

Emily put the broom away and grabbed the sanitation spray. She was still embarrassed by the way she had acted. She had let herself become hysterical for no good reason. She recalled her similar reaction earlier. She wished she hadn't been tricked into this date.

It dawned on her that she hadn't ventured out of town since the day she arrived three months ago. Just before she had arrived, so many bizarre things had happened to her in such a short amount of time that she wondered if it was wise to tempt fate in such a way.

14

Emily - Collision Course

Gemma closed her books and looked at the round clock on the wall, ready to lock up. "Men are always late!"

"I should get home anyway," Emily mumbled. She had every intention of calling the date off half an hour ago when she had finished her duties in the back, but when she had returned to the front of the store to tell Gemma as much, she couldn't help but notice a potted plant had been placed in the window. Her breath caught in her throat, and she found herself unable to tear her gaze from the yellow and green weed that stood upright within it. *Could it be the same one from earlier? Why would someone do that?* The pot itself was trimmed with gold runes, way too elaborate a design for the purpose of transplanting a weed. Emily had only just managed to rip her eyes away from the object as Gemma spoke, startling her back to reality.

"Oh, pish-posh Emily, stop dwelling on that incident at Nina's. It was an accident, and I'm sure Justin forgot about it five minutes after it happened." Gemma placed a reassuring hand on her shoulder. "Come on, I will lock up and wait with you."

As she ushered her out the door, Emily couldn't help but glance back up at the pot one last time to make sure she hadn't been seeing things.

Gemma pointed down the almost deserted street just as an engine roared in the distance. "There he is now, if I'm not mistaken."

Emily followed Gemma's gaze toward the sound just as a battered black and chrome motorcycle appeared in the street up ahead. "Yup, that's him all right!"

Justin pulled up to the sidewalk and planted a foot on the curb as the motorcycle let out a final snarl. A plain black helmet covered his head, and Emily couldn't help but notice that several small dents peppered the plastic safety device.

Gemma laughed. "You are going to ride that old thing?" She placed her hands on her hips and cocked her head at Justin.

"Not to dinner, but I thought Emily might appreciate a ride." Justin turned while still straddling the bike and unstrapped a helmet from behind him. "Then we will go get my car." He held it out toward Emily.

Gemma clapped Emily on the back. "She's all yours. Better Emily than this old girl!"

Emily stepped forward and reached for the helmet. "Right." *This piece of plastic is supposed to protect my brain?*

She looked over her shoulder, and Gemma made a shooing motion in her direction. "Have fun, kids."

Emily squashed the helmet down onto her head and took another step forward as Justin reached his now empty hand out to help her on behind him. Emily hesitated a moment, her hand hovering over Justin's.

"Don't tell me you're scared!"

Emily shook her head as she grabbed Justin's hand.

"Hop on behind me."

Emily lifted one leg over the side of the motorcycle. As she felt

Justin release her hand, she sat down onto the leather seat cover and wrapped her legs around the bike, placing her feet onto the footrests.

The bike roared to life. "You ready?" he shouted. "Have you done this before?" Emily shook her head. "Don't lean with me. Stay neutral. Got it?" Emily nodded in response, and Justin turned to look ahead. "Now hold onto my waist!"

Emily grabbed on just as the bike lurched forward. She heard a clack as her helmet bumped into his. "Sorry," she yelled as she looked over his shoulder, trying to be heard above the engine. But he didn't seem to hear as he pulled away from the curb.

Emily could feel the air rushing past. It made a whooshing noise in her ears, even with the helmet. As they headed away from the town, Justin started to speed up, and she found herself staring at the back of his shirt, pressing her body into his and holding on with all her strength. Emily forced herself to peer over Justin's shoulder and relax her grip slightly. As she watched the world pass by in a blur, her heart rate began to slow.

Soon, trees loomed over them from both sides of the road as they headed deeper into the woods that bordered three fourths of the perimeter of the town. In town, the leaves had not yet begun changing color, but here, orange and red leaves that had dropped from branches swirled and danced off the road as the pair sped past.

Justin slowed to a stop in front of a muddy trail that barely looked wide enough for a small car, and yet Emily could see tire ruts trailing ahead in the soft earth.

Justin lifted the helmet from his head. "Hop off. We can walk from here so you don't get all muddy."

Emily stood and steadied herself by placing her hand on his shoulder as she moved off of the motorcycle.

"How did you like the ride?"

Emily pulled the helmet up over her head and shook her hair loose. "It was nice, but where the heck are we?"

Justin pointed at the trail. "That path leads to home sweet home."

Emily cocked her eyebrow, the strap of her helmet still clutched in her hand as if expecting something to jump out of the tree line.

Justin leaned over the front side of the motorcycle and grasped the handles to push it down the path. "Don't worry, my house is just up ahead out of sight. And we had to come to get the car, didn't we? You can trust me, Emily." He stopped pushing and reached out for her hand. "We will just park this thing and get my car, I promise."

Emily refused his hand but walked on. The trail seemed to be narrowing as they moved forward. The trees were thick, blocking more of the light the farther from the road they went. Emily put her free hand in her pocket and grasped the stone for comfort.

"Emily, it's just the woods. Why do you look so worried?" He stopped pushing for a moment and pointed. "Look up there, you can see the roof of my house."

She realized she had been looking at the ground. There was an incline up ahead, and sure enough, she could see the roof of a house. "Does anyone else live out here with you?"

Justin shook his head. "My parents left the house to me."

"Oh, where did they go?" She realized what a dumb question that was even as she said it. "Sorry."

"No, it's okay. They were in a car accident a few years ago. I stayed in town with my aunt. You know Nina. Until she deemed that I could once again resume living outside of town."

"Nina's your aunt?"

"Well, maybe not by blood. But she's always been my family.

Come on, I can give you a tour ... if you're not too scared." He said it as if he could hear the questions as they formed in her mind.

"I'm kind of hungry," Emily lied.

"As you wish. Car's in the garage."

The garage itself appeared to be clean and organized, although it barely looked like it had room for one more item.

Justin parked the bike inside and hung a small key above it before making his way over to his car. He held open the passenger door and bowed at the waist. "My lady." He motioned for her to take a seat.

Emily placed the helmet she had been carrying down on a wooden shelf above the motorcycle. She gave it one last look before she buckled herself into the car. As they drove down the path, branches hit the doors and scraped across the windows. The sound was reminiscent of nails on a chalkboard and caused her to grimace.

"Still don't trust me, huh?" He looked at her curiously.

Emily turned her face toward him. "Well," she started as she crossed her arms, "you didn't even ask me on a date." She hadn't been the best judge of character in the past, but no one in town had really given her any reason not to trust them.

"Would you have accepted, if I hadn't tricked you into it?"

She looked at him and shook her head. "No, I don't think so."

He gave her a toothy grin. "Then my plan worked out pretty well, didn't it?"

She bit lightly at the inside of her cheek to keep from smiling back at him.

Emily didn't know what she had been expecting as they drove along the deserted road; it seemed to her that they would never reach the forest's edge. She was curious and anxious to see what the town's closest neighbors were like. Emily glanced at Justin to make sure he wasn't looking at her before wiping her sweaty palms on her pants leg.

Just as the trees started to thin out and disappear, Justin swerved to the edge and pulled onto the grass so that the car lights illuminated the field in front of them.

"What are you doing?"

"You didn't seem all that keen on leaving town; I mean, maybe I'm wrong, but I'm usually not..." He popped his door open and walked around the front. Again, he opened the door for her and offered her his hand. "This way."

Emily didn't want to seem ungrateful and accepted as he led her around the back to the trunk. Justin made a waving motion over the trunk with his free hand before exclaiming, "Ala kazaam," and slapping it down on the car.

Emily shook her hand loose to cross her arms over her chest while rolling her eyes.

"What? People say I'm hilarious."

"Sure they do," she said, allowing a giggle to escape.

Jason popped the trunk and pulled out a large brown basket. "Geesh, I made it before I picked you up. Why are you so serious all the time?"

"I'm sorry." She dropped her arms. *Maybe I do need to lighten up.* She placed one hand on her hip. "The fact that you even have a picnic basket, is ... adorable." She covered her mouth with her other hand as she giggled again.

"Hey," he smiled before adding, "I have a picnic blanket too." He scooped the basket and blanket up out of the trunk and walked to the area of the field that was illuminated by the car's lights.

Emily watched, trying to control her giggles as he knelt down and spread the blanket on the grass. "I would turn the car radio on, but you can't really get a signal here." He looked up at her. "Unless, of course, you like listening to a constant drone of radio static."

Emily shook her head as she joined him on the blanket.

Justin began pulling items from the basket, a sudden serious look spread across his face. "I hope you're not expecting a five-course meal." He turned to her and opened the lid of a container filled with assorted fruit pieces. "I really just wanted to get to know you better. I think maybe we have a lot in common."

Emily shifted uncomfortably. "I doubt that," she murmured, chewing at her lower lip.

Justin looked up from the white package he was unwrapping, and as their eyes met, Emily looked away, pulling her knees up to her chest. "Dammit, Emily. I just want to be your friend." Justin's shoulders slumped.

Emily shot him an uneasy smile. "Sorry, I'm not trying to be rude, I just..." Guilt gnawed at her as her words trailed off.

Justin sighed and pushed his hair back from his face. "No, it's okay, I'm sorry. It's just, I have always been different from everyone in town, and I thought you would understand." Justin looked away then turned back. "Never mind, anyway, did I tell you that my motorcycle is one of a kind?" He shot her a cool smile.

She shook her head and sat up straighter. "How so?"

"My father built it before my parents had their accident." Emily cleared her throat, uncomfortable with where the conversation could lead. "Well, I don't have a copy of the plans, so I can't really duplicate it yet... Do you really want to know?"

Emily scooted closer on the blanket, nodding.

"I'm not entirely sure how he did it, but he designed it to be automatic, so you don't have to change gears. I have looked in to it a bit, and I can't find another bike like it. See, usually driving a motorcycle requires much more ... I'm boring you."

She cocked her head to the side. "No, you're not, really, it's just that I don't know much about them."

Justin looked thoughtfully up at the now star-filled sky for a moment before continuing. "On most motorcycles, both your hands and your feet have jobs to do, but on mine, er, my dad's, you only have to worry about signaling, steering, and brakes. I haven't quite figured it out, and I don't really want to have someone else dissect it to find out how it works."

Emily nodded. She understood that feeling. Her arms prickled as an image of herself lying on a table ready for dissection popped into her head.

The wind howled suddenly, lifting the edges of the blanket from the ground. "Em..." Another gust blew across the field, causing the basket to roll onto its side. "We should get going."

She shook the image away and stood just as the rain started to fall. Emily scurried to help retrieve the remains of their dinner. With each passing second the raindrops came down harder, seeping into her clothing. Water seemed to assault them from every direction as they sprinted the short distance to the car.

The splatter of rain against the windshield distorted her view as Justin slowly pulled out onto the road. Drenched and uncomfortable, Emily listened as the rain pelted the roof. The headlights barely dented the darkness in front of them, and she didn't want to break his concentration.

The wind howled again, and Emily let out a shriek as Justin swerved to miss something in the road. She jerked sideways and then forward as he corrected the car's direction.

"Sorry about that, it was just a branch." Justin glanced at her, Emily looked down at her hands, embarrassed by her outburst. "Emily, you shouldn't be embarrassed."

He reached for her chin, forcing her to look up. From the corner of her eye, she caught a glimmer of movement in the distance. Just as she opened her mouth to warn him, the mass collided with the car's hood and rolled upward, causing her to bite down painfully on her tongue. Emily forced her eyes shut and reached out to steady herself as the car spun out of control.

Noises seemed to come at Emily from every direction, her heart hammered against her chest, tires screeched, there was a thud from above, and glass shattered, making a soft plink as it fell onto the interior of the vehicle. She was jerked violently forward again, and then everything stopped. Emily lay there listening to the complete silence with her eyes closed. *I knew I shouldn't have left town.*

Forcing herself to open her eyes, Emily turned her head toward the driver's seat and gasped as sharp pain radiated from her neck with the movement. She groped at it, massaging lightly until the pain subsided. "Justin." She reached up, feeling for the button that controlled the interior lights, and pressed. In the dim light, she could see his chest moving up and down beneath his shirt. "Justin?"

Emily turned to her door, careful to avoid the small, hard pieces of glass that seemed to be everywhere. She lifted the handle and swung it open. Relieved to be free, she stood up and shook glass chunks out of her clothing as best she could before inspecting herself for damage. Content that she hadn't broken or gashed anything, she reached back in and popped open the glove box, sighing with relief at the sight of the bright yellow utility light inside. Emily snatched up the light and flicked it on to examine the car's mangled remains.

The front window had spiderwebbed outward and shattered in several places from the impact. Large indentations on the hood and roof reinforced her memory that something had landed hard and rolled over the top of the car. Emily bent down and pointed her light under the car's frame before continuing around the outside. There was no sign of what they had struck, so she made a wider circle around the perimeter, careful to check the tree line for any signs of disruption.

Emily made her way back to the driver's side door and peered in at Justin. She grabbed at the handle, lifting it up and out. The door didn't want to budge. She dropped the flashlight to the ground and this time gripped the handle with both hands before tugging, but the door refused to open. As she released that handle the second time, Justin let out a pained groan.

Emily snatched the flashlight back up and ran back to the passenger's side of the vehicle where the door still hung open. She leaned in over the seat. "Justin?" She snapped her fingers in front of his face. *Nothing.*

Closer now, she could see that the right side of his face was discolored and swollen. "That doesn't look too serious." Emily tried to inspect the rest of his body for damage.

His left foot was wedged up and twisted sideways under the pedal. The sound of static filled her ears. "Great..." She sighed and looked around. Satisfied no one was watching from the trees, she crouched down as close to his foot as she could and lifted his pant leg slightly. Just above the ankle, she could see an unnatural bulge pressing against his bruised skin. *At least there's no blood.*

The static in her ears had almost grown deafening as she reached forward and gently touched the ruined bone with her fingertips. Emily felt the air swirl around her unnaturally. She released a heavy breath, and pulled her hand away.

It's going to happen, whether I want it to or not. "Shoot, shoot, shoot." Frantic, Emily looked up. "Justin?" It hurt to speak as the energy tried to force its way out. *Still out cold.* Emily placed her hand on the foot and allowed the wave of strange magic to crash out of her and over him.

She felt the bone right itself and snap back into position beneath her palm. Emily lifted her hand up from his leg. Not even the slightest discoloration from the bruise remained.

"All right," Emily said, wiggling back up from the awkward position and turning to face him. Justin's eyes stared intently back at her. Emily's stomach turned. *Did he see?* Her breath caught in her throat. *He had to have seen it.* Her heart started racing. Panic-stricken, she turned in her seat and clutched the flashlight's handle as she jumped from the car and darted straight into the woods.

15

Emily - Expulsion

"Wait, Emily." She could hear Justin calling into the woods after her. "Come back."

Never, she thought.

The moonlight barely shone through the canopy as she continued to move deeper into the woods. *Why do I have to be such a freak?* Tears tickled her cheeks, *I can never go back. He will expose me to everyone.* She pushed through the trees and shrubbery, not caring where she ended up as long as it was far from him.

As the sound of his calls faded into the distance, Emily found it increasingly difficult to detect the outline of the obstacles in front of her, and she was forced to slow down or risk a painful collision. Still, she fought the urge to turn the flashlight on, not sure if Justin had followed her and unwilling to give up her location.

Finally, panting for breath, she collapsed into a heap on the damp leaves. Complete darkness soon enveloped her, and she clutched the flashlight to her chest, ready to turn it on without hesitation if the need arose. *No matter where I go, it will only be a matter of time before the same thing happens again.*

Leaves rustled nearby as the nocturnal creatures of the forest went about their normal activities. *Maybe I can live here in the* woods like a hermit and sneak into town from time to time for supplies. Emily lifted her head, wiping away the tears with the sleeve of her light jacket. No. She didn't want to go back to being a phantom. She couldn't bear the thought of living that way ever again. I managed to survive then, and I can do it now. It will just have to be somewhere else.

It just hurt. Emily had liked staying in town — had even felt accepted. Most of the people there didn't seem to mind that she kept to herself. They were polite to her. Many were even kind. Gemma will be worried if she doesn't hear from me. Somehow, I'm going to have to let her know I'm leaving. Emily turned the flashlight on and stood to brush the fallen leaves from her muddied clothing.

A familiar blue light penetrated the utter blackness ahead. Emily released her grip on the flashlight and let it fall into the soft leaves. The strange glowing ball zigged and zagged around, as if the creature was trying to avoid a collision. She cocked an eyebrow and stared at its movement.

The wisps were not solid but rather some strange living gas or balls of energy. She had seen them pass through solid things. No. Emily crossed her arms over her chest. That's not quite right.

A wisp had moved straight through her hand. She remembered the tingling sensation as it met her flesh. It had happened the first night after she used her gift. The wisps had just been there in her room, waiting for her to lift her head. She had not actually witnessed their arrival. But have I ever? At the hotel, the wisp was already in her bathroom when she opened her eyes.

Emily dropped her arms to her sides as another blue light appeared, moving in the same strange dance. The first wisp had reached her and now hovered innocently at her shoulder. How long have I been running? Her legs suddenly felt like jelly as she lowered herself to the ground. In the company of the wisps, the forest didn't seem quite as dark or as dangerous. Emily looked up at the wisps and whispered, "We should just rest here for a few minutes."

When she looked back up again, she was shocked to see that light had begun to trickle through the foliage. *Did I fall asleep?* No, she had just been staring off, lost in thought. She didn't feel very rested, despite the break. If anything, she felt more worn out than when she had first taken her seat in the dirt. *Is this what whiplash feels like?* She hoped she was never in a car accident again. The wisps still hovered nearby, and she silently thanked them by offering a salute in their direction.

She pushed herself up off the ground before turning in a circle to take in the sight of the woods that seemed to stretch out for miles in all directions. She reached up to the sky and then down to touch her toes, hoping to loosen the muscles in her lower back and neck.

"Emmmily…" A faint voice reached her ears from the distance. *Justin. How could he have found me?* It felt like she had run for miles. "Eeemily."

Frantic, she looked for a place to hide. Emily inspected the tree closest to her, studying its branches, and frowned. Activities like climbing trees had never been her strong suit. She faced the wisps; there was a chance she still could elude him.

"Emmillyy..." The voice was getting louder. She was sure of it. He wouldn't give up.

"Help me," she whispered. The wisps circled her once then jetted away from her, farther into the wooded expanse. Emily moved to follow, not really looking at her surroundings as she rushed to keep up. Running in the dimly lit woods was even more disorienting than in the pitch darkness of the night as obscure green and brown shapes seemed to pop from nowhere into her line of vision. Emily had to duck at the last second on more than one occasion as huge branches suddenly sprouted inches from her face.

As she passed beyond the barrier of trees, she was temporarily blinded by the bright light of the rising sun. She stopped and bent forward with her hands on her knees as she sucked in several deep breaths. Once she caught her breath, she looked up, shielding her eyes from the morning rays.

The wisps had stopped just beyond the forest's edge, beside Justin's house. Emily slapped at her forehead and spun around to face the wisps. "Oh, come on!" But the wisps were gone. She kicked at the ground in frustration. She had to get out of there.

Emily stepped into the garage. The motorcycle key still dangled from the hook on the wall, right where Justin had left it. She grabbed a helmet and lifted it onto her head.

"Just like riding a bike." Emily bit into her lower lip as she reached for the handlebars and kicked up the stand. The weight of the motorcycle strained her arms as she slowly pushed it out of the garage. Justin had made it look so easy.

Once on the dirt path, Emily found that she had to push forward with all her weight against the heavy bike, digging her shoes into the mud as she went. It was a tedious trek, and she frequently glanced over her shoulder, expecting Justin to appear even without the roar of the engine to alert him of her presence. By the time she managed to get the bike to the road, her thighs burned from the effort.

At the road's edge, Emily gripped the handles and straddled the bike, placing her feet on the rests. She turned the key and positioned her fingers onto the brake and clutch levers before looking ahead at the deserted road.

Emily bit into the now raw flesh on her lip. *Okay, left hand, clutch and the turn signal, right hand, brake. Twist the throttle, make a turn, how hard could it be, right?* She let out an exaggerated breath as the engine roared to life. *Just take it slow..*

It took her a little while to figure out how to keep the motorcycle balanced. At the first curve she tried to go around, she forgot to move her body with the bike. The descent seemed to happen in slow motion; the bike continued crawling forward as it leaned too far to the side with Emily still firmly on the seat. She screamed out in pain as the bike pinned her leg to the road. She could feel the heat of the metal through her pants, burning at her leg, as she squirmed out from beneath the heavy metal beast. She gritted her teeth as she heaved the motorcycle up to get back on.

Emily dumped the bike on its side in front of her building and darted up the stairs and into her room. No one shouted up after her, and she was relieved that the house seemed to be empty. She peeled off her stiff shirt and replaced it with a fresh one. A door slammed from somewhere below. Emily looked at her mud-caked jeans. *No time.* Instead she tore a sheet of paper from her notebook and scribbled a letter to Gemma. *It will have to do.*

She pulled open her drawer and removed whatever cash she had managed to save from working, then made a circle in the room she had called home for the last three months. It was much the same size as the bedroom she had stayed in at her parents' home, and yet life here had been so different. The red backpack she had carried with her from the pool still hung from a hook by the door, in the same spot she had placed it when she had arrived.

Emily slid her hand into the pocket to grasp the amethyst for comfort. Instead of the stone's smooth surface, she felt only the coarse and gritty mud-caked material of her jeans. The pocket was empty. Her jewel must have fallen out. She had to go back for it. She tried to trace her steps through the wood, never really believing she had dropped it there. Couldn't have. Because there would be no way for her to go the exact same way she had before. The search would be useless. It could easily be hidden under

135

leaves. She had to believe it was in the car.

Lack of a good night's sleep was starting to wear on Emily, and she yawned loudly even as she maneuvered the machine into an upright position and slid onto the seat. The engine didn't scream in response as she turned the key; instead it sputtered and went silent. She turned the key back and tried again. The motorcycle coughed and squealed back at her before it finally let out a loud roar. She lifted her feet from the ground and headed back to the scene of the accident.

The car was gone; the only sign of the collision that remained was a few fragments of glass on the pavement. Emily walked along the tree line to the spot where she thought she had entered. She scanned the woods unsure of what direction to go. *This is hopeless.* She walked back to the edge and peeked in, trying to visualize which direction she had been traveling. *Completely hopeless.* Emily breathed in the earthy scent of the forest. The amethyst had never been so far out of her reach. Since she had come to possess it, the gem had become her security blanket.

Emily lowered herself to the ground. Most of the forest floor was covered in a colorful blanket of leaves. She hadn't taken a moment to think since she had run. The tightness in her chest had grown throughout the day, and now that she was no longer in a state of perpetual motion, she felt she could barely breathe from the weight.

She had felt this tightness before, but it had never grown so excruciating. *Where will it go If I try to push it out? What will happen if I don't?* Emily thought of the man that had attacked her and how he had fallen to his knees in front of her. When the static sound filled her ears, and she had released the pressure. He had scared her, and she had known it would stop him.

Another memory resurfaced, one from the night of her eleventh birthday, only hours after she had healed the bird. She had sat propped up against her bedroom door, confused by her mother's actions and hurt by her words. Emily recalled the thud she had heard on the staircase, like someone was pushed against the railing, followed by her mother's startled cry of pain. She had felt it then too, the strange tightness. Just like at the hotel. Only that time the wave that had released from her had been directed at her mother. A tear trickled down Emily's cheek, and she wiped it away. *It doesn't make sense*; her mother hadn't died, and she was fairly certain that Mr. John Doe had.

Emily stood and clenched her fists. A large, moss-covered rock became her target as she tried to force the static wave to surface from inside her. She grunted with the effort to push the energy outward. She kicked at the ground with her foot at let out a strangled cry as she dropped back down to the forest floor in a heap.

The leaves she had kicked up were matted and dirt-covered. The darker brown shades looked odd against the bright colors of the freshly fallen leaves that surrounded them. Now that Emily had something to look for, she moved around carefully, examining the forest floor for similar signs of disruption. Excited by the prospect of recovering her amethyst, Emily ignored the tightness in her chest and resumed her search.

Knowing new leaves would have fallen during the day, she paid special attention to the areas where broken branches dangled directly above a patch of disturbed ground. As she ventured deeper into the trees and the foliage became thicker, the evidence that she had run through was much easier to find. Emily frowned at the site of a tiny pine she had inadvertently uprooted in her haste to get away from Justin. She bent down to examine and rebury its roots before moving on. A short distance later, she stumbled upon the large yellow flashlight. Having sat in the spot, Emily took extra time to feel around the ground for the stone, sifting through the leaves and forest debris. Her heart jumped into her throat as a flash of fur scurried over her outstretched hand. She sat back on her heels and took a deep breath.

The culprit, a little brown mouse, had only scurried a few feet away and now sat up on its hind legs, staring toward her. Its whiskers and tail seemed to twitch in unison as it let out a squeak she could barely hear. Emily smiled. "Sorry. If it makes you feel better, you nearly gave me a heart attack." The mouse let out another annoyed squeak and then turned away from her. She watched, waiting for it to run off, when something suddenly went flying past her head, so close she heard a swoosh sound in her ear, a blur of silver and the flash of claws. Again, her heart went into her throat, and this time it brought the sound of static.

By the time her brain registered the large, round eyes of the owl for what they were, it was too late. The unsuspecting bird let out a bloodcurdling squawk as the wave of energy rushed out of Emily and washed over it.

Emily knelt beside the bird. "I'm so sorry."

The owl was gray with black dusky spotting that speckled its body, almost like that of a snowy owl, but it had silvery feathers scattered amongst the rest that shimmered when the light hit them. Its eyes opened, looking right at her, but it made no move to attack or cry out. Emily could see that one of its legs and claws were twisted around unnaturally on one foot.

Despite the danger of handling an injured wild animal, Emily was determined to take the owl for help. She reached her hand forward to caress its feathers; the owl only blinked at her in response. Emily got the impression that the owl was not afraid of her at all. She carefully slid both arms under the bird and gently lifted it. She then turned one elbow out to cradle the owl, as she had her dolls when she was a child. Satisfied the bird was as comfortable as possible for the time being, she began looking for evidence of the path she had taken the night before.

16

Amanda - Strange Premonitions

Amanda was surprised to find herself in the dream place. Aden hadn't brought her there in a long time. She breathed in deeply the sweet scent of the wildflowers all around her. She pivoted on her feet until she could see the craggy tree in the distance and concentrated on it, envisioning it moving toward her. Getting around like this was necessary in the dream place, and she had done it so many times before that she barely had to think about it. The action had become automatic for her.

She looked up into its twisted branches, admiring how full it looked when it was covered in white and pink flowers. She had a sudden craving for its exotic golden fruit and wondered if Aden knew when the tree would bear apples again. The fruit didn't just taste good; it also numbed pain. *Knowing when to harvest them could prove useful,* she thought. Amanda leaned against the tree's rune-carved trunk, confident that this would be the first place Aden would look for her.

He had only left to take Kiami to the Human realm a short time ago, and she questioned if it was possible that he had sensed her already having second thoughts about the mission she had sent them on. She shrugged off the notion; it was more likely he had known she would be restless from the moment they were out of her sight. Either way, she was happy to visit the familiar place.

Where is he anyway?

"Aden?" She stood straight and called again, louder. "Aden?" Not even the wind whispered back in response.

Amanda took a deep breath and let it out in a slow, deliberate manner. Dreams were not always safe, and not all of her experiences here had been nice. The memory of icy crystals snaking up her body caused the hair on the back of her neck to prickle. The unnatural frost had immobilized her limbs as it climbed, rendering her defenseless.

What if someone or something else brought me here? She leaned forward and yelled as loud as she could, "ADEN?"

Dread filled her. This place had its own set of rules, and she wasn't sure she knew them all. In the past she had only ever been brought here by Aden or Erol, and after they left she would have nothing to keep her tethered to the dream.

Unless it's not a dream at all... Amanda reached over her shoulder and touched one of the scars that stretched across her back. Traveling through realms took strong magic, she knew. The seven runes that had been carved there were her painful reminder. The realms had been created to stop the different magical races from reaching one another.

I'm being illogical.

She moved farther from the tree and looked out into the field.

"Hello, is anyone out there?"

She thought she saw the faint shape of something moving in the grass. She squinted hard. Whatever it was seemed like it was getting closer, but the image remained clouded.

"Can you hear me?" she called once more, waving her hand in the air. Another figure came into view, far to the right of the first.

Amanda lowered her arm. *What is going on here?* A third blurred humanoid figure emerged from nowhere, and then another.

She took a deep breath. Part of her was curious about where they were coming from. The other part of her was relieved that they didn't seem to be able to hear her. She folded her arms in front of her. Six of the out-of-focus characters now roamed the field. They each appeared to have two arms, two legs, and a head, but beyond that Amanda wasn't able to make out any distinguishing features.

She forced herself to look away. It wasn't the first time she had witnessed something ominous here. She considered that the apparitions could be lost or looking for something. *But that wouldn't explain why I'm here. Could Kiami have given up already and told the town's inhabitants of my plan?* Amanda didn't think so; her new spy had seemed excited to learn about Emily and the jinn.

She lifted her eyes back to the field. There were still six cloudy figures, but they no longer wandered about. They stood in a perfect semicircle, and Amanda would bet that if she could see their faces, they would all be turned toward her.

She thought she saw the images flicker, and she rubbed at her sore eyes. *Have I been squinting this whole time?* She kept them closed, waiting for the stinging to subside. When she opened them again, she was met by her own reflection. She was once again sitting at her small, mirrored table.

17

Emily - The Cost of Magic

After wandering for what felt like hours with the still bird in her arms, Emily approached the edge of the tree line. The sight of Justin's house made her both anxious and relieved. She would have to take her chances. Her arms felt heavy as she made her way into his garage, and she longed to set the bird down, if only for a few moments.

The mangled car and the bike that Emily had abandoned beside the road were both parked inside. A wooden crate rested on its side between the vehicles that looked about the right size. Emily smiled at the animal and shifted it into one arm before pulling the back door of the car open and grasping for the picnic blanket. She knelt down beside the box and flipped it upright so she could pad the bottom with the cloth. Satisfied she had done all she could to comfort the bird for the moment, she laid it inside, whispering, "Just give me a few minutes."

Emily stood and turned back to the car. She had to believe her stone was somewhere inside. The glass had been cleaned out, and she hoped Justin had done a good job as she ran her hands along the seam and down under the cushions.

"Tsk, tsk, tsk, Emily." Justin leaned against the door that led from the interior of the garage into his home. "Looking for this?" He lifted his hand to reveal the missing amethyst.

Emily stood. "Give it to me." She balled one hand into a fist.

A smug look spread across his face. "Why, so you can steal my motorcycle again?"

Emily relaxed her hand and dropped it to her side. "Please." She stepped forward. "I don't want to have to take it from you, Justin."

Justin furrowed his brow. "Then don't, Emily." He stood fully upright. "Come inside."

Emily backed up a step. "No."

Justin slid the gem into his pocket and moved into the garage. "I don't know what to do to make you believe me, Emily." He raised his empty hands as if to show surrender. "You can trust me. I will not hurt you."

"No, but you can try." Emily took another step back and bumped the crate where she had laid the owl. She let out a shriek as the box leaned to one side and then landed back in its correct position. Emily went down onto her knees to make sure she hadn't caused the bird more harm or frightened it with her clumsiness.

She reached inside to stroke the owl's head. It still didn't shy away from her touch. Her cheeks burned as she stood again to face Justin. "Give me back the amethyst!"

"Dammit, Emily." Justin kicked the door frame with his foot. "If I give it to you, will you come in and talk to me?"

Emily looked down at the owl. The bird stared back at her and blinked once. *Maybe he will know what to do for her.* She bent down to pick up the box. "Fine, but only because I need your help."

"Come here and get it," he said playfully.

Her sore arms screamed in protest as she hefted the box up onto her hip to carry it into the house.

Justin wrinkled his nose and watched her. A spark of curiosity danced in his eyes. "What in the world are you doing?"

"I told you," she said, straining under the weight. "I need your help." She pushed past him into his kitchen, wondering if she was making a terrible mistake. She chewed at her lower lip as she slid the box onto the countertop.

Justin peered inside the crate then backed away, grinning. "Why do you have that wild animal in a box. Are you going to sick it on me?"

"Stop. It's not funny." Emily leaned over the box again. "I hurt her, and I need you to help me fix it."

Justin moved back to the crate and reached in slowly, touching the feathers on one of its wings lightly. "What do you mean you hurt it...?"

"I can't explain right now. It just happened. There is something wrong with its leg. It can't walk. The poor thing has to be in pain!"

Justin leaned over the crate, studying the bird. "I wonder why it didn't fly away." He cocked an eyebrow. "Why don't you just fix it?"

"I can't." A tear trickled down her cheek.

"You fixed me, didn't you?" Justin put his hand on his hip. "Explain."

"I told you I can't. Just please, help me, help her."

"Okay, okay. Let me go get the first-aid kit from my bathroom." Justin spun around the corner, and Emily heard his heavy footsteps on a staircase.

She reached back in and caressed the bird's feathers. "I'm so, so sorry."

Justin's head popped back around the corner. "How do you know it's a girl anyway?"

Emily looked up. "I don't. I do... it... she just is, okay?"

"All right, all right." Justin reached into the box and slowly pulled the owl out.

"Be careful not to bump her injured leg."

"Don't worry, I got her." He turned his head to look back at her from over his shoulder. "Follow me this way, nurse."

Her eyes were trained on the owl as Justin carried it into the next room and around to the front of his sofa. She hovered, watching from behind the long L-shaped couch as Justin knelt down on a blanket he had spread out over the floor.

She held her breath as she watched him gently place the bird down onto it. The owl remained almost completely still as Justin popped open the top of his first-aid kit and took out supplies. The bird's eyes seemed to follow him as he wrapped its leg in several layers of gauze.

"I don't think I have ever seen a wild animal that was injured be so tame."

Emily gasped. "Why? Do you think there's something else wrong with her?"

"No, shush. Calm down. I mean, I am not a veterinarian, but she seems okay. She is just not acting how I would have expected." Justin looked up at Emily. "I thought I was going to need you to wrap her in the blanket and hold her."

"Maybe she is someone's pet."

"Maybe." Justin jumped up. "Watch her, don't let her move."

Emily heard a bang and the clatter of something falling to the kitchen floor.

"Dammit."

"Do you need a hand?"

Justin appeared back in front of her. "No. It's fine, I really needed to reorganize that drawer anyway." He held up two popsicle sticks. "These look about right." He returned to his position on the floor and carefully held the sticks to the bird's appendage.

He reached around with his free hand and dug through the kit until his fingers landed on a roll of white binding tape and slowly started to wrap it around the sticks to form a splint. "Can you dig the scissors out of that box?"

Emily located them and knelt to snip the tape just as Justin finished his last layer of wrapping.

"Perfect." He moved the blanket around the bird like a nest. "Okay, Em. That's the best we can do for now."

Emily stood back up and looked around the room. Behind the couch, a metal spiral staircase jutted up into the ceiling, and in front of the couch, built into the wall, was a large fireplace with a smooth stone facade and mantel. Emily looked longingly at the fireplace as a chill ran through her. She rubbed her arms to warm them.

"Are you cold? You're shaking."

"Yes."

"It's supposed to frost over tonight. I should have started the fire." He smiled and turned toward the fireplace, bending down to ignite the flames. "Want some cocoa? I mean, I know it's a kid drink. Guess I never grew out of it."

Emily smiled. "I would actually love some."

He stood and motioned for her to follow as he made his way back into the kitchen and pulled a chair out for her at the table. "M'lady."

Emily sat in the chair with her chin resting in her hand. *How can he be acting so normal?* she wondered. *Maybe he didn't see, and I just ran off like a basket case and stole his motorcycle...*

Within minutes, Justin returned carrying two mugs overflowing with whipped cream. "I know, ridiculous." He grinned. "There's some marshmallows in there too." He placed a spoon in front of her.

"No, it's great. Thanks." Emily swirled the sweet concoction together with the utensil, dreading what would come next. *Might as well get it over with.* "So what did you want to talk about?"

Justin raised his eyebrows, and she looked away from him, once again sure that he had seen.

"Okay." He put his hands up. "Emily, I don't care how you did it. Please. I am glad you did. Who wants to wear a cast for weeks? Trust me, it sucks. I have had to before."

She stared down into her still full mug. *He really sounds sincere.*

"I haven't told anyone," he reassured her. "Although when Gemma heard my car was towed, she called me, worried about you. News travels fast around here."

Emily looked back up at him, searching his eyes for any sign that he meant her harm. "Where did you say I was?"

"I told her you were shaken up after the accident and sleeping here on the couch." Justin stood up and pulled the amethyst from his pocket. He stared at it hard for several seconds before finally placing it down in front of her. "I knew you would come back for that." He plopped back down into his chair and leaned forward, examining her eyes. "What did you do to the thing that crashed into my car?"

Emily sighed. "I was hoping you knew what happened to it, or at least what it was ... it was gone when I got out of the car."

"Emily, are you in some kind of trouble? Is that why you came here, to this town, I mean?" He moved to reach for her hand, but she pulled it away, hiding it on her lap beneath the tabletop.

"It's what everyone's been wondering."

She looked back up at him then, startled. "What do you mean everyone?"

"It's hard to explain right now, later ... it would be easier if I knew what you are."

Emily jumped out of her seat. "What do you mean, what I am? Isn't it obvious? I'm cursed, that's what I am!"

Justin remained in his seat and took a sip from his cup, gulping loudly as he swallowed. "No, that's not it at all. Can't be." Just as he opened his mouth to speak again, a large crash reverberated through the house. Justin jumped up from his seat and ran around the corner.

Emily followed as far as the bottom of the staircase and watched as he bolted to the upper floor. She turned toward the couch, her eyes resting on the blanket where the bird had been. All that remained were torn fragments of the makeshift splint. Emily chewed harder at her lip as she searched the rest of the room for the injured bird.

Justin reappeared on the stairs. "I must have left a window open. It's really blowing good outside. The lamp didn't stand a chance." He paused halfway down and eyed Emily suspiciously. "What are you doing?"

Emily turned to look up at him as he slowly finished his descent. "She's gone!" She lifted the tattered remains of the splint and held them up for Justin to see. Then she lowered her arms and looked at the floor. "She's just gone..."

Justin took slow strides toward her. "The owl?" He lifted her chin with his hand. "I told you it was odd that she didn't try to fly away. She probably flew out the window upstairs."

"Well, what if she only tried to fly out the window?" A tear streaked down her cheek.

"We will go out and look." He released her chin. "Let me rephrase that. *I* will go out and search the yard. You look exhausted."

"But it's my fault! It's always my fault." She looked down at her feet. "I have to help."

"You can be the most help right now by getting some rest. I'll go look, but remember, Emily, that owl is an animal, and if it was able, it probably just went home. You, on the other hand, look like you haven't slept in days. I do have an extra bedroom upstairs, and you are welcome to sleep there if you want, or you can lie down on the couch by the fire."

"Right here is fine." Emily sat down hard on the sofa and stared into the orange-and-blue flames, watching them flicker and dance. Moments later, Justin appeared in front of her wearing a heavy coat. He carried a thick blanket in one hand and a lantern in the other.

He set the blanket beside her. "I will be back soon."

Emily pulled the heavy blanket over her as she heard the door bang shut, then she gazed into the glow of the fire.

18

Emily - Fierce, Fiery Friends

Emily awoke to the smell of frying food and the sound of whistling. She slid off the couch and onto her feet, meaning to apologize to Justin. As she entered the kitchen, her words caught in her throat at the sight of the shirtless figure in front of her.

"Take a picture — it will last longer."

Emily jumped at the sound of his voice. Caught, embarrassment flushed her skin as he turned toward her. "Did you find her? The owl, I mean?" she stammered.

"No. I looked for an hour. There was no sign of her anywhere. I'm sure she's safe somewhere healing." He took a few steps toward her and leaned over to grab something from the counter. "Sorry, it's like eighty degrees in here." He slid the shirt over his head. "When I got back from town, your teeth were chattering."

"Wait, you went into town last night? And you didn't think to take me home?" Emily reached for the door handle. "I need to go. I'm sure Gemma is missing me at the shop."

Justin grabbed her by the hand. "Now you just hold on. You're always running away. In fact, I am pretty sure if you hadn't dropped your rock, I would never have seen you or my motorcycle again. Can't you just stay and listen for ten minutes?"

"Fine." Emily yanked her hand lose and folded her arms in front of her. "I'm listening."

Justin waved a spatula in the air. "That's better. Now, first of all, Emily it's six o'clock. You have been asleep for almost twelve hours. Gemma would have closed up shop an hour ago. Second, you obviously needed the rest, since I did try to wake you up before I went to talk to the council, but all you did was mumble gibberish at me. I thought maybe there was something wrong with you. That's why I went to talk to Gemma."

Emily looked at the floor. "Gemma knows I'm cursed?"

Justin's smile faltered. "Oh, don't start that again. Things like this are hardly ever what they seem to be." He set down his spatula and fiddled with the knobs on the stove. "So, I went to talk to Gemma, because I'm not a doctor, and she instructed me to let you wake up on your own. Then she scolded me for allowing you to wander around in the forest night and day."

Emily couldn't help but smile. *That definitely sounds like Gemma.* Still, her stomach twisted at the thought of him telling her everything he had seen. "Justin, who is this council, and what exactly did you tell them about me?"

Justin reached out for her hand. A smile danced in his eyes and spread across his mouth. "Come with me. I have to show you something." He pulled her into the living room and stood beside her, facing the hearth.

Justin extended his arm toward the fire and gestured for her to come closer. The fire began to move and morph into a long, snakelike tendril. Emily took a step back and sucked in her breath. The tendril flickered as it stretched out of the fireplace and upward as if it was a living creature. Justin waited unflinching as the flame snaked forward, wrapping itself around his hand and making its way up toward his shoulder.

She bit at her lower lip as she watched the flames reverse back down Justin's arm and condense into a ball in his palm. He leaned his face down toward his outstretched hand and blew gently onto the fireball, which sent it floating off his hand and back into the fireplace. Emily moved forward to search him for evidence of burns or even scorch marks. But just as she reached out for him, Justin was gone.

She couldn't stop the shriek from escaping her lips as an invisible arm wrapped around her waist, sending chills throughout her body. Emily found herself unable to raise her voice above a whisper. "Justin?"

"Emily." A hot breath exploded against the back of her neck as the faint voice reached her ears.

"I think you made your point." She breathed. "Let go." She felt his arm slip away, and she moved forward, crossing her own arms over her chest. The fire still burned in the hearth, and Emily stared thoughtfully into it, aware that Justin had rematerialized and was looking at her, expecting her to say something else.

She heard him step up behind her. "It's not the same thing, you know. I realized something when I was out there in the woods... Every time I heal something, someone else gets hurt. It's like a sick joke."

"Is that why you said you hurt the owl?"

"After I heal someone, there's this pressure... It's like when I fix someone or something, I take the negative energy and carry it with me, but eventually it has to go somewhere else." She felt Justin's hand grip her shoulder and turned to face him. "It needs to be expelled."

He gazed into her eyes. "You're not alone anymore, Emily. We can all figure this out together."

Emily took a step back. "All? Are you saying there are more

people like you in the town?"

"Yes and no. Let me explain. Come sit down."

"My mother was a human, and my father was a jinni." Emily opened her mouth to speak. "Just hold your questions for a minute and listen." Justin adjusted himself in the seat so that he was facing her. "It is something that shouldn't happen, because the jinn do not reside in this realm long-term, or aren't meant to anyway. But you will hear more about that at the meeting tomorrow."

"Meeting?"

"Yeah, just wait, okay." Justin scratched the back of his head. "It's funny, I couldn't get you to say two words to me, and now I can't get you to stop talking." He winked and smiled. "My father didn't know exactly what to expect when I was born. To him I looked like a human child, and to put it simply, younglings do not. My father knew that even though I looked like a human baby, there was a very high probability that I would, at some point, manifest some jinn abilities. Now, younglings' behaviors and how their talents manifest can be highly unpredictable and often impossible to control, at least until they mature to adolescence. So, for my protection, my parents brought me to this town for refuge. Unfortunately, it has a barrier of sorts, and one purpose of this barrier is to deflect mundane beings. They wouldn't die if they came into the town or anything, but if they did manage somehow to stroll on through, they would feel real uncomfortable doing it. It's sort of the first line of defense, meant to protect humans just as much as the jinn that live there. It's also the reason my father built our house outside of the town limits, so that we could live together, the three of us, as a family." Justin sat back against the couch cushion.

Emily's smile faltered as she rose from her seat, taking his silence as a cue to speak. "So, you're saying that we are alike because neither of us seems to belong anywhere?" She began to pace the room. "And the meeting is to, what, decide if they are going to kick me out?" She paused, wondering if she should run again. "You're at least somewhat like them, Justin. You're half jinn." She turned to the door, still contemplating another hasty retreat.

Before she could act, Justin reached up and grabbed her arm. "No, Emily listen. You're misunderstanding. The town meeting is for you. The jinn that live there want to officially welcome you." He released her arm and looked up in to her eyes. "I don't know what happened to you before you stumbled into our town, but Emily, you will be safe here."

"I will stay for the meeting." Emily hadn't been the best judge of character in the past, and her stomach was in knots. She wanted to believe Justin and trust the people here, but she wasn't even sure what jinn were. Questions swirled in her head, and the only way to get the answers would be to stay.

Justin clapped his hands and grinned. "I'm so glad to hear that. The washroom is upstairs. Why don't you go get cleaned up and come join me for dinner? I cooked, after all."

Emily glanced down at her filthy clothing and grimaced. "I would like to go home and change."

Justin's smile faltered. "Gemma kind of asked me to keep an eye on you until the meeting."

"She doesn't trust me."

"No Em, it's just a lot to take in..." He reached up to rub the back of his neck. "And with everything that's happened in the last two days, I felt kind of responsible. I volunteered to keep an eye on you. Not that you need a babysitter, it's just..." He trailed off and looked back up at her. "There are still some of my mother's things here. I'm sure I can find something you can use."

Emily studied her reflection in the mirror above the sink, as she had just days before. The only noticeable change was the dark circles that ringed her eyes. She scrubbed her face and hands before reaching out to grasp the soft yellow material of the sundress Justin had left for her. She slipped the dress over her head and looked back into the mirror. The shade of the dress seemed to exaggerate the color of Emily's eyes so that they appeared to glow back at her.

Justin was standing at the table, scooping vegetables onto

plates as she rounded the corner into the kitchen. "There you are. For a minute I thought you decided to crawl out the window and down the drain pipe." He smirked, then looked up from his work to add something but quickly snapped his jaw back shut as he inspected her from head to toe.

Warmth spread across Emily's cheeks as she moved past him to sit. Once she was securely in her seat, she cleared her throat. "Thanks for dinner."

Justin pulled out his own seat and looked down at his plate. "I will have your clothes ready for you before we leave for town." The words sputtered out of his mouth.

Emily moved the food around on her plate with her fork. "Is something wrong?'

"No, you just look so ... different. I'm sorry."

Emily pulled the blanket up to her chest and looked at the fireplace. All that remained were some bright embers that glowed and flickered as they fought to come back to life. Justin's words, *Things like this are hardly ever what they seem to be,* reverberated in her head.

The town looked deserted as they pulled onto the main street. Emily was relieved as she hopped from the motorcycle. She was still nervous about what the people here would think of her and the things she could do.

"Everyone is in the diner." He motioned for her to follow, and she reluctantly walked to the front door. Justin raised her chin with his hand, forcing her to look at him. "It's going to be okay." He let go of her chin and reached for her hand, holding it tightly as he pushed the door open.

This was either going to be the happiest birthday of Emily's life or the saddest.

She squeezed her eyes shut. She couldn't stand the thought of seeing Gemma and Cherry look at her in fear and disgust as her mother had. Her heart raced as Justin guided her forward a few more feet and then stopped.

"Open your eyes."

Emily shook her head, still clutching his hand.

"There's no one here anyway," he added.

"Is that another one of your jokes?" she whispered.

"Do you hear anyone?"

She relaxed her grip on his hand and bit her lip as she listened. She heard nothing beyond the low whirring sound of the ceiling fans overhead. She opened her eyes and dropped his hand. "So it is one of your tricks then."

He didn't respond as she scanned the empty diner. A folding table had been placed in the center of the aisle that ran between the rows of booths. It held a large, rectangular cake. Emily took a few hesitant steps forward and then stopped. Two words were written in purple icing across the top of the white frosting.

"How did you know?"

"I didn't." He stepped up beside her. "That sort of thing is Gemma's specialty."

"Making cakes?"

"Hardly." A look of amusement spread across his face as he shook his head. "Knowing things."

"Like how you manipulated that fire?"

"Yes, jinni can have many different magical abilities. But it is important to remember that there are also a few common traits we all share."

Emily looked at him and rolled her eyes as she remembered the way he had vanished and snuck up behind her. "Tricky Justin, very tricky." *The residents of the town have been here the whole time.*

Gemma and Cherry were the first to reveal themselves, and within minutes every booth appeared to be full.

19

Kiami - Advantages for Owls

Kiami hadn't realized that Emily was like a powder keg ready to explode.

For the few days that she had been watching, she stayed hidden in owl form.

It hadn't been long enough for her to understand Emily's abilities, and she had only seen her heal Justin. She should have realized there would be some ... repercussions. After all, there always were in myths when magic was involved.

Now that she knew, she almost felt like a kindred spirit, and it had been her own fault.

She should have eaten something well before she let the owl's natural predatory instinct kick in. The idea of eating mice didn't entice her, but she was starving, and when the mouse sat out there in the open, Kiami couldn't resist. She was so preoccupied with the mouse that she hadn't even noticed that Emily was also watching the vermin.

As Kiami swooped down for the gray morsel, the blast from Emily drove her backward. A sudden intense pain caused her to falter. The forest floor was covered in layers of leaves, but they did little to soften the blow. She lay there, momentarily stunned, not really understanding what had happened. She had never felt a magic attack aimed at her before. It reminded her of the way the ocean crashed against the shore near her home.

When it ended, her leg was twisted and mangled. She could have changed right then and been spared hours of pain. But she wasn't ready to reveal herself to Emily. She let her wings flop out limp from her body and froze in place, waiting to see what Emily would do.

Kiami was sure no one could fake the wide-eyed look of concern that remained on Emily's face as she hauled her up from the ground and into her arms.

She found that she really didn't like being carried around, but she couldn't come up with a good way to get Emily to put her down, and she certainly wasn't going to peck her. Emily's persistence after hours of searching for a way out of the forest, in her rather uncomfortable state, only made Kiami like her more.

When they arrived at Justin's, he was harder to read. Kiami thought perhaps he was just as confused as she was, until she saw a twinkle of something in his eye. Kiami could tell that he knew there was more to her than just the owl that lay broken on his floor.

Maybe I should be grateful that he didn't blow my cover. I heard their conversation. If he was trying to earn Emily's trust, why didn't he just out me?

Kiami had removed the bandage with her beak while they were engrossed in their uncomfortable conversation in the kitchen. She could really understand where Emily was coming from and wanted to know more. But her leg was pulsing with pain in a way that was starting to make it hard for her to concentrate.

She had slowly limped her way up the staircase, which was no easy feat. Owls can't turn doorknobs very well. She was panting by the time her owl body reached the top.

Justin had left the window open on purpose, she supposed. When she got back to the cover of the trees, she transformed into her human self and healed for the most part. Only a dull ache remained.

Afterward, she sang as she wandered, not out of necessity but to lift her spirits. Something from nature was feeding her, and she could feel the remaining pain begin to ease. She had always liked singing before the incident with the boy...

Other than the native plant life, there were no living creatures in sight. Not knowing where she was draining the energy from caused her to slap her hand over her mouth and stifle her melodic singing. She didn't want to feed too much from whatever it was and decided to change back into owl form.

She perched high up in a pine, facing Justin's garage. Kiami closed one eye. Exhausted, she was grateful to be able to get some kind of rest while she waited for them to leave again. If she had a mouth, she would have been smirking; one of her favorite advantages of being an owl was the ability to remain alert while sleeping.

Anyone that wishes harm wouldn't be able to just wander into

town... That's what Justin had said. Kiami couldn't help but wonder if it was true. She had been sent here by Amanda to spy, after all.

Kiami followed, out of sight, as the pair sped into town on the motorcycle. She was not surprised when her feathers seemed to tingle with an unusual energy as she swooped down over the main street.

Kiami flew away from the pair, trying to keep her distance as the motorcycle came to a halt in front of a restaurant. She made a large circle back toward the grassy town square. It seemed to be at the very center of everything that the one stoplight town had to offer.

Kiami landed on a bench, bracing herself in case of another unknown magical attack, but nothing stirred around her. She turned her flexible owl head. Most of the businesses across the street were dark in all directions. From what she had overheard while she was at Justin's house, the sight of the empty town didn't surprise her.

The townspeople had waited months to show themselves to Emily; of course, everyone would be at her welcoming ... *party? Is it a party?*

With her exceptional vision, she had no trouble seeing from this distance, and although she couldn't make out what they said before Justin pushed the door open and they moved inside, she had noted the way Emily hesitated before entering.

Kiami hopped from the bench and wandered toward the monument at the square's center. Around the trunk were seven carvings that she had seen before. The image of the scars on Amanda's back had been burned into her memory. Angry scars like that could only come from pain.

She had no doubt that Amanda had endured the things she had

claimed, but she had to come to her own conclusion about the town. She couldn't just pass judgment on them so easily, the way Jacqueline had judged her the last time Kiami had seen her.

The jinn had not been directly responsible for the things Amanda had endured, and she had yet to see proof that these townsfolk harbored any great secrets beyond being jinn in the Human realm.

Kiami continued on, walking with her wings slightly raised in case the need to fly arose as she made her way toward the building with the white-and-red awning that Emily and Justin had entered. She needed to be closer if she wanted to hear what the townspeople had to say.

The diner was filled with an exited chatter as Kiami attempted to get her balance along the thin windowsill. Just as she managed to find a comfortable position, pressed close to the glass, the chatter stopped.

A voice drifted up from the quieted group. "Do you have any questions, Emily?"

She must be so nervous, Kiami thought.

"I am wondering..." She heard Emily clear her throat before continuing. "Justin said that jinn aren't meant to live in the Human realm. If you don't mind me asking, how did you all end up here?"

The sound of rustling leaves close by caused Kiami to tilt her head back away from the window. She peered out toward the center of town for a moment watching for any sign of a breeze. *Tree statues don't have leaves that rustle, silly.* She knew even with her spectacular hearing, there was no way she could have heard wind moving through branches from outside of the village.

Something wasn't right. She hopped from her perch and scanned the town. Muffled voices rose once again excitedly from inside the diner, and she tilted her head back in the direction of the window, but she was no longer close enough to make out the words.

The sound of steps on the pavement moved away from her, and she turned her head around in search of the cause. A shadowy figure slunk a short way ahead of her, shoulders slumped and head down. She cocked her head to the side. *How could someone have walked by me?* She flapped her wings once in frustration. *Darn it.* She wished she could sigh, but an owl didn't have the ability. Instead she clacked her tongue against her beak.

Kiami set a course and slowly crept after the figure. There weren't many places available to duck down out of sight, even as an owl. The specter leaned into a building as if trying to push a door open and then walked a few feet farther before repeating the action. This time the door opened, Kiami could hear a gentle squeak from its hinges, and she hurried to catch up.

She looked at the brick building squashed between the antique store and the five-and-dime. The door hung open, and a "Closed" sign swung back and forth on the knob. A dim light glowed in the room beyond the entrance, and she ducked inside, keeping a sharp ear out for the intruder.

Piles of books and magazines were stacked on the floor, and Kiami moved behind a row of them before peeking around the side.

Beyond her hiding place, rows of half-filled shelves lined the small bookstore.

A newspaper rustled, and someone cleared their throat as Kiami squatted back farther behind the stack.

A raspy woman's voice called out. "Your ability to be unseen doesn't work inside of town." The newspaper rustled again, and a brighter light sprang into the room. "How can I help you, boy?"

Kiami peered above her hiding place, releasing a relieved breath. More books and magazines lined the counter where the woman sat, the newspaper still clutched in one hand and a steamy cup in the other. A half-cocked smile played on her lips. She was not looking at Kiami but at the shadowy figure, who seemed to be shivering.

An arm raised to its head as it was pushing hair out of its face. "Come now, boy, surely you have no reason to try to hide yourself from a fellow jinni? Although you're starting to make me wonder."

Kiami heard the woman's cup go down unto the countertop, and Kiami glanced back at the woman. She now stood with her hands pressed firmly onto the counter. A scowl had spread across her face.

"Okay, okay," a familiar voice responded, and Kiami snapped her head back around to see Aden where the specter had been.

Kiami took a step backward. *He's not supposed to be here.* She inched her way over to another stack of books to get a better view as Aden approached the woman.

"I'm kind of lost," Aden said, fingering a stack of maps on the countertop. The woman was looking at him her mouth now a thin line.

"Lost? Are you sure you're not exactly where you mean to be?" Her eyes were questioning.

His smile dropped, and a noticeable shiver ran through him. "I'm not sure a map will help."

She leaned across the counter. "No, I'm sure it won't."

Suddenly there was a whirlwind of movement from the doorway as two women rushed in.

Kiami moved farther backward, barely registering the feel of the bookshelf pressing into her feathered body as she watched the newcomers grab Aden and pull him through a door she hadn't noticed before.

The woman behind the counter stood upright and turned her head toward Kiami. She lifted her arm and pointed to the door. "Out now."

Kiami's heart raced in her chest as she stumbled forward to obey. In her panic, her wings felt like dead weight dragging on the floor as she scurried out onto the sidewalk.

20

Kiami - Eyewitness

Kiami sped across the street as fast as her owl legs could go, her sharp nails clicking against the gravel. Part of the sidewalk across from her opened up unto a large field and Kiami continued out into it.

Her bare feet went down onto the cool bed of grass. The unexpected sensation on her skin brought her to a stop. At some point midrun, she had transformed herself back into human form without even realizing she had done so. She turned around and stared back at the small village, her breath coming in short pants. From here, she could barely see the outline of the buildings that made up the town.

Kiami sank to the ground and looked up at the night sky. Unanswered questions danced around in her head. She needed to think, but first she had to get a hold of herself. A stream babbled quietly somewhere close by, and Kiami lay back, allowing the thick grass to tangle around her.

This is all wrong. Aden is not supposed to be here. And neither was the unicornesque creature that collided with Justin's car.

She had already spent plenty of time thinking about how she had stumbled upon Emily.

Tripped over, more like it, Kiami thought.

The whole mission had seemed utterly impossible to begin with, like looking for a needle in a haystack. Armed only with Emily's name and a few bits of information about the town itself, Kiami hadn't felt very well prepared when Aden left her on the deserted road. She was not a tracker, let alone a spy. But a deal was a deal, and she had wanted to try.

Rain had begun to pour down on them as they said their goodbyes, drenching her. Even after he had disappeared from view, she remained in human form as she enthusiastically made her way down the dark road on foot.

Kiami enjoyed the kiss of the raindrops on her skin and the dense, earthy smell that arose from the ground, enveloping everything within its embrace, just as she loved the feel of the earth on her bare feet.

She gazed up at the purple haze of the night sky, her feet never missing a step. The light of the stars was hidden by the shadows of the rain clouds. This mission was the beginning of something new, an adventure, and it sent a tingling sensation down her spine. She now understood better her mom's excitement at exploring the unknown.

If it weren't for her exceptional hearing, she probably wouldn't have noticed the strange, repetitive noise from somewhere in front of her. The sound echoed even in the storm. It was as if someone was clicking their tongue repeatedly in the darkness. At first, she could only make out a dark, fuzzy, distorted shape.

She stopped moving and stared ahead, squinting in the direction she heard the sound coming from. She was usually a pretty good judge of distance even in the dark, but she was having trouble focusing her eyes.

A chill crept up the back of Kiami's neck as a gust blew, causing the branches to bend and wave on either side of the road. Her adventure had suddenly turned into a nightmare.

The creature had only needed a few seconds to pinpoint her location. Its ears forward, it let out a whinny and a screech before lowering its head as it charged toward her.

In owl form, rain posed a different problem for Kiami. Her feathers were barely water-resistant, and she knew it would quickly become hard for her to navigate an escape.

Kiami turned to flee, changing as she ran, but there was a new blur of movement in front of her as she spread her wings and pushed herself up from the road quickly.

Behind her, the creature let out a snort as it leapt to follow.

It wasn't until she heard the loud thud and the screech of tires as a car spun out of control that she had realized the vehicle must have intercepted her pursuer.

The rain stopped just as Kiami glided into the canopy of the forest and perched herself at the edge of a branch to look out at the scene. She could see the battered car below, but the creature was out of sight.

Kiami waited several minutes, watching the car, listening to the rustling in the branches and the slight howl of the wind. She had wanted to make sure that whoever was inside was all right, but she couldn't bring herself to get closer.

She knew what she thought she had seen, and at the time the urgency to flee had been so strong that she hadn't doubted herself for a moment. But things like that didn't live in the Human realm.

If not for the wreckage that had been left behind from the impact, Kiami would have believed the whole incident had been a hallucination, possibly a side effect from traveling through the realms or the product of an overactive imagination and stress.

By the time Kiami had convinced herself that the creature was nothing more than a deer all along, the passenger had gotten out of the car and begun to search around outside. Kiami watched her movements, sure the girl would see something that she herself had missed.

It was the driver's groan and the sight of the panicked girl racing back around the car that had finally forced Kiami to summon the courage to move closer. She had, after all, caused the collision.

The car had swerved to a stop at the edge of the forest, and Kiami lifted her wings before pushing herself from the branch. She glided, maneuvering to the ground so she would remain hidden behind in the overgrown vegetation.

Kiami had been wondering just how she could help with the injured driver when she had picked up a low static noise, something she had noticed while she was at the castle with Amanda. Something a human ear would never have picked up at this distance.

It was too much of a coincidence for Kiami to believe. What were the chances that the very person she was supposed to be looking for in the village had shown up on this very road at this time?

Kiami had been too stunned to move at first, even after Justin jumped from the car and shouted after Emily.

21

Amanda - Dreams and Schemes

For Amanda, the days after Aden and Kiami left had passed slowly. She was unable to keep herself sufficiently occupied, and the nightmares returned with a vengeance.

"They have captured him, you know..." Abaddon's voice was like venom. "You must prepare for the worst."

"You lie." She closed her eyes tightly, not wanting to believe what she had already suspected.

"Yes, well, it is true that I can't manifest myself directly into the jinn village ... yet, but I do have an anchor there. Right in the middle of town. I watch them on occasion, and I see things."

"What exactly did you see?"

He let out a half snort, half grunt and stared down into her eyes. "I can *see* that you're losing control. I can help you get it back. You must embrace your inherited power."

She responded through clenched teeth, "Even if I believed what you said, my shadow magic is too unpredictable."

He patted the top of her head. "Amanda, always thinking of the many, even after all that you have been through. You could learn a thing or two from Kiami. Did she even question what you were after? No, she was only thinking of what you promised to do for her."

It was true that Kiami had not questioned many of the things Amanda had told her, and now she couldn't help but wonder if Kiami had known more than she let on all along. *What if she has her own ulterior motive altogether? It couldn't hurt to be prepared.* "What do I have to do?" Even as she said it, a sinking feeling filled her stomach.

"The solution lies in your memory. Do you recall the rune-carved tree from the dream world?"

Amanda nodded.

"If you bury an item of power at the roots of the tree, it will offer you one of its branches, a branch that if used correctly can help funnel your energy." He moved around her seat and looked into her eyes. "It needs to be both something powerful and symbolically important to you. I'm sure you have something lying around in that castle of yours."

Amanda thought of the dagger that Jacob had created so long ago to capture Aden and wondered if the memento was powerful enough to work.

"You will be able to concentrate your power more precisely and hold better control over the shadows. It's really a small price to pay."

She shook her head as she spoke up. "I don't know how to get to the dream world on my own."

"That doesn't matter. The trees are symbolic. Their roots tie the realms together. Bury an object under one, it is buried beneath them all."

Amanda's stomach lurched as the memory of her father snapping photos of a craggy rune-covered tree burst free from her carefully constructed vault.

"The runes carved into the tree were familiar, yes? You only need to know how to get to one of the trees."

An earlier memory from that day bubbled up, her and her father sitting at the table. Excited for their upcoming adventure. "Remember Amanda, be ready..."

"For anything," her former self quipped.

Amanda gave one quick nod in response to his question. Suddenly the cost didn't seem small at all.

The very idea of returning to the place where it had all begun for her, even if only for a few moments, made her want to throw up. As her eyes fluttered open, the bile rose in her throat. She quickly leaned over the side of her bed.

22

Kiami - Defector

Leaves rustled on branches in the gentle morning breeze. Kiami let out a sigh as she sat up in the grass, her skin wet from the dew.

The memory of what had happened to Aden had been playing over and over in her mind. With no way to summon Amanda, she was going to have to appeal to Emily for help. She pushed her long, dark hair out of her face and sighed again.

From here everything seemed still in the town; it would be the perfect time to go back and find a place to watch for Emily.

As Kiami moved to push herself up out the grass, a low, throaty growl arose from beside her. She froze in place halfway to her feet and scanned the thick weeds.

Something wet and furry grazed her outstretched hand as the noise came again. "Grrrrrwlll."

She swiveled her head in the direction of the sound, but there was nothing there. Damp fuzz tickled at the bare flesh of her heel.

Whatever was threatening her, it couldn't be very big. Kiami pushed herself the rest of the way up. "Grrrwllll," came again, just as she caught a dark brown blur of movement out of the corner of her eye.

Kiami breathed sharply inward as the creature appeared in front of her.

"Grwwlll." The seemingly solid ball of fuzz was no bigger than a cantaloupe. Four stubby legs were barely noticeable amid its long fur. Kiami remained still, trying to gauge its intentions, unsure whether to smile or run. Its tiny round button-like eyes stared back at her, unblinking.

Then, with a sudden movement, its whole face tilted upward as if its mouth was on a hinge at the centermost part of its circular body.

A shrill yip-yip noise emanated from the creature as it began to dart around her, faster than even her powerful eyes could keep up with.

She thought of the wisps and how she had reacted before hearing about Amanda's encounter with them. She had certainly misjudged their intentions. Later in the woods, Emily had asked them for help. It was clear she had been both familiar and at ease in their presence.

Kiami bent back down and extended her hand into the bizarre critter's path, and the blur of movement came to a stop again in front of her.

She couldn't hold back a smile as the creature snapped its wide toothless mouth closed and began to hop from foot to foot as if it was overcome with the prospect of some attention.

Kiami took a hesitant step forward and scratched its head. "You're kind of cute." He leaned into her touch like an attention-starved pet. She knelt down and let the critter climb into her lap. "Where did you come from? Or what did you come from?"

The animal's eyes smiled up at her as it opened its mouth. This time, a long, white tongue unfurled from within and flopped out sideways. "You're a peculiar little thing, but if you can believe it, not the weirdest thing I've bumped into lately."

His fur felt like the fibers from a cotton plant ready to burst. She gave the critter a delicate squeeze. "What am I going to do?" The smile melted from her face. "I could run away from here, but if Amanda found me once, she can do it again, and I can't just abandon Aden."

The fuzzball wriggled at her touch. "Do I even believe that the people in the town would hurt him?" She lifted the animal up and looked into its eyes. "Do you think he is really in danger?" The critter let out a high-pitched yip and slurped at her face, leaving behind a thick, slime-like residue.

"Eww. Thanks for that." Kiami placed him back into her lap and wiped at her face. "Why should Emily help me anyway? She doesn't even know me, and what if she realizes I have been spying on her..."

The animal nuzzled against her stomach as she began petting him again. "You know what? There's no use jumping to conclusions, is there?" She gave him another soft squeeze. "I'm glad we had this chat." Kiami continued to caress the animal. "I don't suppose you have a name. How about fuzzball? Or fluffy?" Kiami shook her head. "No, I will have to think on it."

The critter wriggled out from her hands and stood on its little legs. It turned to face the field away from town, letting out a low growl as it moved.

Kiami followed its gaze, trying to catch sight of what had stolen her new friend's attention and put it on edge.

The air had filled with a thick haze, as if it was a humid summer afternoon instead of the barely lit early morning. Apart from the infrequent rustle of leaves in the distance and the constant low babble of the stream, all was silent.

The fuzzy lifeform growled again as it rolled forward off her lap before darting out into the peculiar shimmery mist, a smear of brown that quickly disappeared from her view.

Kiami cupped her hands around her mouth and shouted out after him, "Until we meet again." The critter hadn't given her any answers, and yet she felt better, lighter as she hopped back to her feet and made her way toward town, humming as she walked.

At the sidewalk's edge, she paused and studied the layout. The monument in the center of town looked like the perfect place to keep an eye both on the shop Emily worked at and the bookstore where she had last seen Aden.

From the ground, Kiami hadn't noticed the long, thick thorns that had been carved to jut out from the highest limbs. She was careful to avoid them as she settled into the branches of the stone tree. The branch felt peculiar to Kiami. It was cold and smooth beneath her, instead of the rough bark of a natural tree. Her skin crawled as she involuntarily lowered the front of her body, stretching her head low and forward.

Instinctively, the feathers on her head, back, and flanks bristled, and her wings extended slightly as if a threat approached. Poised for attack, she fought to hold in a warning screech as she jumped from the branch to abandon her post.

Kiami tilted her head and looked back up at the tree. The feeling of unease had followed her to the ground. Something just wasn't right. The streets still appeared to be empty, and yet the threat seemed to be all around her.

Her doubts returned afresh. It suddenly seemed dangerous to be surrounded by so many magical beings. Kiami spun her head to get another glimpse of the still town. She had never felt so out of sorts in owl form before. Her throat was tight, and she could feel her heart beating against her chest in a frantic rhythm. Powerless to hold the screeches in any longer, the high-pitched noise exploded from her beak.

Unable to focus on the prospect of flight, she hobbled forward, trying to escape the danger as another screech ripped its way out. Kiami pushed her small body ahead into the street, wings still outstretched. She had almost made it to the edge of town before her wings finally obeyed.

23

Kiami - Snooping

Kiami peeked around the side of a large oak that grew at the edge of the thick, wooded area bordering Justin's property.

His whistling could be heard above the sounds of running water and clinking dishes from inside.

She continued to listen as she stepped into the sunlight, moving toward the house and through the attached garage.

As Kiami gave the door several quick raps with her fist, the noises came to an abrupt stop.

Within seconds the door swung open. Justin barely glanced at her as he turned to place a plate into an open cupboard. "I was wondering when you'd be back." He pulled the worn dishtowel from his shoulder and tossed it onto the countertop before spinning around to face her.

Kiami took a hesitant step back from the door. "How did you know?"

Justin grinned slyly. "Well, I didn't, not for sure, until now," he added as he took a step toward her. "It's a small town, and there's been a lot of gossip since last night." He leaned forward over the threshold and plucked something from her hair. "And then there's this." He displayed a small silver feather, twisting it between his fingers.

It was rare for them to come loose, but it wasn't the first time one had been left behind after a transformation.

Kiami gave a quick glance back over her shoulder, wondering if she could clear the opening of the garage before he could catch her. "Will they be coming for me then?"

Justin lifted an eyebrow. "Who?"

"The jinn from town..."

His other eyebrow went up, causing his forehead to wrinkle. "Because you flew into a bookstore and knocked over some shelves?" He released the feather, and Kiami watched as it floated down to the floor.

Clearly the gossipers had negated Aden from their story and left her the sole culprit ... but why? "That's what the gossip was about?"

"I hear you startled the heck out of Mrs. Nazari ... and I am sure she startled you right back. Gemma and Cherry were over there for hours cleaning up." Justin planted his hand on his hip. "Why do you think they would be looking for you?"

Kiami shrugged. *Maybe it would be best not to mention Aden for now.* "Can I come in, please?"

Justin stepped aside. "Sure, be my guest."

Kiami heard the door close as she made her way to the couch, smoothing out the thin white material of her dress as she sat.

Justin teased. "Make yourself at home..."

Kiami half smiled up at him. "Sorry." She extended her arm toward him, offering her hand. "I'm Kiami."

He accepted her hand, giving it a light squeeze before releasing it. "Justin," he gave her a quick wink, "but you know that already, don't you?"

Kiami looked down at her hands and gave a slow nod.

"So, do you want to tell me why your here or..."
Kiami threw him a sharp look. "I was sent here to find Emily."

Kiami stretched out on the small bed. Justin had insisted she stay and rest in the guest bedroom, and although she wasn't tired, she was glad she had agreed.

The old wooden toy box that was pushed against the wall opposite her suggested that this had been his room when he was a child. She had lifted the lid and stolen a look inside before making her way to the bed and discovered it was filled with old toy cars and motorcycles.

The room had recently been painted and the aroma lingered, filling her nostrils. The room looked fresh and clean, but empty. A small pile of framed pictures lay on top of the dresser, awaiting either rehanging or storage.

She rolled to the side and pulled up the edge of the dark blue bedspread to peek underneath. Only a single open top shoebox was visible. Her hair flopped down and brushed against the floor as she reached for it.

Clutching the side of the container in her hand, she wiggled the front half of her body back onto the bed and placed the box beside her.

Photos lined the top, and Kiami began pulling them out one by one and examining them. The first few were of a man and a woman. As she pulled out more, a baby appeared between them. Then a toddler. With each additional photo she inspected, the child morphed a little more into a kid-size version of Justin.

Her own growth pattern hadn't been so predictable, and she found herself fascinated as she reached for another, but instead of a thick, smooth photograph, she grasped a handful of coarse handwritten pages.

Kiami glanced at the box, hoping for more photographs, but the only item that remained was a small square package, wrapped in shiny metallic paper.

Disappointed, her eyes flitted over the pages. They were letters to Justin, private letters of condolence. Kiami's face grew warm with embarrassment.

She had saved similar items after her own mother's passing, and the idea of someone foraging through them made her stomach turn. She straightened the letters and restacked the photos in order before sliding the box back under the bed where she had found it. Kiami let out a sigh and jumped up from the mattress.

There was just one small glass porthole in the room, and she shuffled her feet as she made her way over to it. The round window pushed open easily, and Kiami poked her head out to breathe in the fresh air.

She didn't believe Aden was in any immediate danger, but she was eager to get proper introductions with Emily out of the way.

24

Emily - Belonging

Dazzling sunlight flowed in through the window, streaking across Emily's face. She groaned and covered her head with her pillow.

She had lain in bed most of the night, staring at the ceiling, questioning her new reality and contemplating her reasons for allowing herself to be hidden away for so long...

The party, the walk home — it had been so much to take in, she hadn't managed to fall asleep until the first few rays of dawn peeked into the edges of her window.

The haze of sleep hadn't completely lifted, and Emily felt herself drifting back away.

A sudden thundering knock caused her to clench the pillow tighter. She whispered into the dull white fabric, "Please go away."

Everyone knew Gemma had given her the day off. Her boss had made a point of announcing it before she and Cherry had left the party, and with the exception of Mrs. Nazari, the entire town had been squashed into the diner for her welcoming.

Memories of the restless evening brought a smile to her face. Gifted or cursed, she was accepted here, and it had been the first time since her eleventh birthday that she had fallen asleep feeling truly and completely safe.

Emily reluctantly pulled herself up from the bed. "Coming, I'm coming..." She dragged her feet as she moved to the door, rubbing at her half open eyes with her palms.

The door creaked loudly as she pulled it open and lifted her face to the visitor.

Justin grinned back at her from the other side. "Rough night? Dreaming of me, I hope?" He waggled his eyebrows at her.

Emily glanced down at her wrinkled clothing and then back up at Justin, rolling her eyes when they met his. "Is this important?"

Justin leaned against the open doorframe and brushed his hair back with his hand. "Your owl friend showed up at my house. I thought you might want to come by and see that she's okay."

Emily cocked her head to the side and furrowed her brow. "I'm too tired to determine whether or not you're joking." A yawn forced its way out of her mouth with the last word.

Justin's usual mischievous grin morphed into a straight line as he straightened himself and crossed his arms over his chest. "I'm being serious, and yes, I think this is important, actually."

Now what? She bit at her lip as she took a step back from the door. *This visit has to be about more than just the owl.* She had never seen Justin wearing such a stern expression. Even when they were discussing her powers and the town, he had seemed somehow lighthearted. "I'll meet you downstairs in five minutes."

Emily swung the door shut and stretched her arms toward the ceiling. She released another yawn and glanced around her room. A grin crept onto her face, stretching from one side to the other as she whispered, "I belong here."

She splashed some water into her tired eyes and hurried to pull on some clean clothes before bounding down the stairs two at a time.

Outside, Justin waited at the passenger side of an unfamiliar car. As she approached he bowed to her before pulling the door open.

Emily was relieved to see that a smile had found its way back onto his face, and she giggled as he added, "Your chariot awaits," gesturing for her to get in.

"New car already?"

"I borrowed it in case I needed to bring you girls back to town later."

She rumpled her brow as she looked at him from her seat. "Don't take this the wrong way, but sometimes I don't get your sense of humor."

Justin gave an exaggerated shrug before closing the door. Emily watched as he made his way around the car and into his own seat.

By the time they reached his driveway, Emily had counted six instances where he had turned to her and opened his mouth, only to snap it shut again without saying a word.

Something is worrying him. Emily patted her pocket. She had almost left the amethyst at home, but grabbed it just before walking out the door.

Justin grasped her shoulder as she pushed the door open, and Emily turned to face him. "She looks ... different than the last time you saw her."

Emily gasped and narrowed her eyes. "You said she was fine!"

"Shh, no that's not it. She is perfectly healthy, I just..." He looked down and brushed his hair back with his hand. "You will see."

A groan escaped Emily's lips. "You're cute, but sometimes you're so frustrating. Now I don't know if should be relieved, excited, or worried!"

Justin slowly raised his eyes back up to meet hers before flashing her a toothy grin. "Wait, you think I'm cute?"

She turned away and leapt from the car, slamming her door shut behind her. "And frustrating!"

She chewed at her lip to keep herself from smiling as she waited at the entrance of the house.

Startled, she bit down a little too hard as his voice called to her from inside. "She was upstairs in the guest room last I knew."

Justin had sailed past her without making a sound. *Guess I will have to get used to that,* Emily thought.

Emily poked at the newly forming bump with her index finger.

"Well at least my lip isn't bleeding," she muttered under her breath.

"What's that?"

Her heart jumped in her chest as Justin spoke from behind her. "Please stop doing that," she squeaked.

"Sorry. It's just, well, she's not here, I checked all over inside." Justin shrugged. "I'm sure she didn't go far; she came to us for help."

Emily shook her head at him in disbelief. "I'm not even going to ask."

Justin spun on his heels and headed toward the door.

"Now where are you going?"

"She's probably just in the woods. Are you coming or what?"

The edge of Justin's methodically trimmed yard was littered with an array of exotic debris, and Emily bent down to pick up a palm-sized red petal. It felt velvety soft between her fingers as she held it up in the sunlight. "What kind of flower did this come from?"

"That, maybe." Emily looked toward the tree line, where Justin pointed at several waist-high plants that bore the same heart-shaped petals. All around them, prehistoric looking ferns poked out from the wood's edge, mingling with the other more familiar plant life.

She stared beyond the outlying flora and into an alien forest. Something about it had changed. The woodland had been brimming with life before ... now the area itself seemed even lusher, fuller than she remembered, as if the vegetation had doubled overnight.

An organic smell of rotting compost rose up with the swirl of the wind, causing a tickle in her nose, and she pinched it at the bridge, trying to quiet the urge to sneeze.

She watched, bemused, as Justin pushed past her and into the mutated forest.

"Are you sure that's a good idea?" She took only a few hesitant steps forward to follow. "Have you ever seen anything like this before? Maybe we shouldn't rush in there."

Justin's eyes danced with curiosity. "Oh, come on. It will be an adventure. Let's go find your owl." She stayed put, watching as he turned in a slow circle. "Never seen anything like it before."

Fallen branches and fruits lay scattered and rotting on the ground. Bright-colored mosses of reds and blues the likes of which Emily had never witnessed clung to the rocks and trees.

The air felt heavy, and an eerie hum reverberated all around her, dampening the shuffling noises of foraging animals from deeper within the interior.

Justin raised his hand over his shoulder and signaled for her to follow.

The farther she stepped, the more mystical it seemed. The sprawling trees reminded her of watchful guardians hovering over their charges, and a shiver flowed through her. Huge roots jutted up out of the ground, rising high above them before they came twisting back down into the dirt, creating malformed arches.

Emily stopped dead in her tracks and spun on her heels. She had lost sight of Justin. She clutched at the amethyst in her pocket before calling his name.

As if in answer to her voice, the heart-haunting melody of a song split the air, calling to her, beckoning her deeper into the center of the woods.

She was helpless to resist as her arms and legs began to move with the rhythm while propelling her gracefully forward through the bramble and weeds.

Try as she might to listen, the words were unrecognizable to Emily's ears, yet the whispered syllables spoke to her just the same, and she understood that the song promised if she continued onward, it would reveal a dark secret to her.

The song made her feel giddy as it continued to move through her.

A sudden forceful pressure snaked its way around her waist, causing Emily to release a high-pitched scream of outrage. She jerked as her arms and legs fought to move forward. "Let go," she managed to blurt as she struggled to free herself.

Still, the thing grasped firmly on to her, tightening its grip on her torso. Her mind raced; with every second that passed, the need to move toward the song seemed to double.

Her breath caught in her throat and her vision blurred. "Breathe, Emily." A voice echoed from somewhere nearby. Like the forest, the voice seemed both familiar and foreign at the same time.

She shook her head in response to the unseen face. There was no time to breathe; the song called to her and she needed to "Move..." She groaned through the pain in her chest and stomach. "Let go," she wheezed.

The melody became fainter, and her heart fluttered in her chest as she strained to find the song again.

"It's me. Stop it, Emily." The voice shouted into her ear from behind. *Justin's voice.* "What are you doing?"

Emily struggled to answer, to remember what she had been do-ing, but her thoughts felt as hazy as her surroundings appeared. She closed her eyes and tried to focus. The last thing she could see clearly was turning in a circle and finding him gone...

Her throat felt sore as she spoke. "There was singing..."

Justin pulled on her arm as he knelt, and Emily allowed herself to crumple to the ground next to him.

"I won't leave your side again, I promise." He reached for her hand and gave it a quick squeeze. "Do you remember where you were going?"

She shook her head. What she thought she had heard in the music was too crazy to repeat. "There is something wrong with the forest."

Justin hopped up onto his feet. "Maybe there is... And that's all the more reason not to leave Kiami alone here."

Emily tilted her head to the side. "Who's Kiami?"

Justin reached up and rubbed the back of his neck. "Kiami is the owl."

A smile played on Emily's lips. "You named the owl?"

He shuffled his feet impatiently and extended his hand to help her up. "No, she already had one. Can we just go look for her?" he added as he pulled her to her feet.

"Well, maybe you should try calling her name then," Emily quipped.

Justin shot a smile at her before closing his hands around his mouth in a circle and shouting the name into trees. "KIIAAAMII, KIAMMII."

Emily reached up and tugged at his sleeve. "Is this whole thing some kind of joke?"

He turned to her before dropping his arms back to his sides. "No, let's look over there." He nodded toward a sword of supernatural light that poked through the canopy.

Emily reached for his hand and gripped it, pulling his arm toward the shaft of lustrous gold light.

As they stepped into the illuminated area, Emily let out a sigh. There was nothing extraordinary here; it was just more of the same. "Can we go back now?"

She had hoped that once they got this far, Justin would be satisfied with the search and call it off.

Justin looked down at his feet and shook his head. "We aren't looking for an owl. Well, we might be but..." He lifted his face to meet her eyes. "Kiami is a girl, like you."

"Like me?" Emily backed up a step and felt the rough bark of a tree press against her shirt.

"Well, not exactly like you, no. I just thought it would be more fun to wait to explain until you met her." He looked back down at his feet. "Boy, has that backfired."

"So that's why you said she already had a name? She's a girl that turns into an owl?"

Justin gave her a quick nod.

Emily's face felt flushed. She slid her back down the tree until she was sitting up against it. "You should have told me. Everything is not a joke, Justin."

He gulped loudly and looked up. "I know, I'm sorry."

Emily pointed to a bright blue pillow of moss in front of her. "Does she have anything to do with this?"

As if on cue, a small, lizard-like creature rose up from the plant and took flight. Its blue coloring had allowed it to perfectly blend in with the moss, and Emily watched in silence as it seemed to pirouette in the air before turning its slit-pupiled eyes toward her.

Emily gawked at the small, winged creature as she took in the sight of its swishing tail and flaring nostrils. Without taking her eyes from the creature, she whispered, "This thing doesn't look happy with me, Justin."

The four digits on each foot ended in a sharp claw, and Emily gulped as the image of them tearing into her flesh entered her mind.

She pressed a palm into the dirt and collected a handful. As she prepared to jump up and throw the dirt in the creature's direction, a strange slurping sound came from behind her.

Her heart jumped in her chest as she tossed the dirt forward. In the same instant, something white whizzed past her face and wrapped itself around the animal before it could lunge out in front of her.

"What the..." Justin had finally spoken, but she could barely make out the words over the sound of her heart beating against her chest.

Emily pressed herself more firmly against the tree as she watched the long, slimy tongue contract once around the small, unmoving creature, before it snapped quickly backward, taking its snack with it.

She pushed her index finger against her lip, signaling for Justin to be quiet as she moved to inch her body around the tree trunk.

A thin-figured young woman smiled as she looked down toward the ground. Her straight black hair cascaded around her face as she bent over at the waist to collect something in her arm.

Emily snapped her head back around to address Justin. "I think I found Kiami."

Justin pushed himself up from the forest floor, and Emily followed him as he made his way out of the brightly lit patch of trees. "Kiami?"

Kiami turned, cradling what looked to Emily like a giant ball of fur in her arms. Her hair shimmered with streaks of silver, even in this shadier part of the forest.

"Justin, Emily." She beamed as she caressed the fur ball. "Meet Fizzle."

She gracefully approached them and extended one arm out to Emily. "It is nice to finally be able to talk to you."

Emily gave the hand a weak shake, eying Fizzle. Four stubby legs peeked out from beneath Kiami's arm, and two tiny black eyes could just be seen amid the fluff on its face. "What is that thing?"

Kiami shrugged back at Emily. "Does it matter? That little dragon didn't look too friendly to me; I think he just did you a favor."

"Dragon? So you've seen those before?"

Kiami shrugged again completely enamored with the critter in her arms. "No, but what would you call it?"

Emily twisted one of her curls with her fingers. "I guess dragon does seem right ... but what about Fizzle?"

"We met once before, haven't we, you odd, adorable thing!"

Gag me, Emily thought as she turned to face Justin. "Can we go now?"

He had been staring intently at Fizzle before she spoke. He looked up at Emily and shot her a fast smile before speaking. "Yeah, let's go ... Kiami come on, you have to talk to Emily, remember?"

"I will be right behind you two," she said without looking up.

"Actually," Justin added. "Why don't you lead the way?"

Kiami looked up. "What?"

"You're going to have to put your friend down and show us how to get out of here."

She gave a nod and looked back down at Fizzle, tickling his fur.

Justin folded his arms over his chest and gave a grunt. "Kiami, now, please." His voice was stern, as if scolding a child. "Put him down."

Kiami leaned down to release him from her arms, a pained look on her face.

She didn't look back at them as she began the trek. Emily

grabbed at Justin's arm. "I think you hurt her feelings," she whispered. "Why were you talking to her like that?"

"She is so ... detached. She didn't seem like herself, and I think her pet had something to do with it."

"Oh, you know her so well after one day?"

He pushed his hair back with his hand and shook his head. "Maybe I'm wrong. Let's catch up, and if you don't agree with me later tonight after you talk to her, I will apologize."

Emily twisted at a strand of her hair and gave him a nod. "Let's get out of here."

25

Emily - The Barefoot Spy's Tale

An awkward silence had settled over them since they had arrived at Justin's house, and Emily shifted uncomfortably in her seat, waiting for Kiami or Justin to start the conversation.

Justin sat with his chin resting in his palm. His eyes had a glazed look as he gazed into the unlit hearth, lost in his thoughts.

Emily chewed at her already sore lip and averted her attention to Kiami, whose feet appeared perfectly clean, despite the fact that she had been wandering around the woods with nothing on to protect them.

She had noticed that while they were still making their way out of the forest, and although Kiami hadn't seemed to be bothered by the rough terrain at all, Emily couldn't stop herself from cringing every time she watched the girl step on a pile of rocks or a fallen branch.

Kiami appeared to be staring out into the kitchen. Emily watched as she lifted a finger to her mouth and began to bite at her nail.

Vanessa would have called her an odd bird, for sure, Emily thought as a thin smile spread across her lips at the memory of her friend. *She certainly never would have stood for such a stiff encounter. She would have been making faces or whispering jokes in my ear to make me laugh...*

Emily wanted to break the ice. She turned her whole body to face Kiami and reached out to grab hold of her free hand. She looked up into Kiami's strange eyes and in the most monotone voice she could muster said, "You know, if you're hungry, Justin is a pretty good cook."

Kiami pulled her finger from her mouth and examined it, as if she herself hadn't been the one to gnaw the nail down past the point where it met the skin. "I haven't chewed at my nails since I was small," she muttered.

"Nervous habit?"

She shook her head. "Not a nervous thing, more of a reminder thing ... I like to sing, only the music was inside of me before I could even speak."

Emily lifted an eyebrow. "You like to sing?"

Kiami stood up to face them both. "From the moment my mother thought I was old enough to understand, she warned me about singing around people, so I started biting my nails when we had company as a way of stopping myself. I loved to sing, I think I may even need to ... and it was hard for me to understand at first why I couldn't, or rather why I shouldn't."

She spoke with a new confidence that Emily hadn't witnessed since meeting her, and she wondered if this was part of what Justin had been referring to in the woods.

"My mother said she would often go to my room to verify I was real, only to find the maids standing within my door and around my crib, unaware of what they were doing. Swaying to the slow, soft sound. There were no words, of course, but a humming melody was all it took. They wouldn't leave; she couldn't snap them out of it until she or Jacqueline quieted me. She said the dazed looks on their faces told them enough. As I grew, the radius of the affected area seemed to get larger, and sometimes I would accidentally cause people from the beach to wander up unwittingly unto our property, leaving them standing perplexed in front of our home."

Emily nodded at Kiami, understanding blooming within her. "You can control people when you sing. They are drawn to you."

"I..." She cleared her throat. "I've never really spoken about this to anyone besides my mother. But I think I needed to tell you. I feel like I am finally starting to make the right decisions since losing her."

Kiami's eyes seemed to twinkle back at Emily, and with one graceful movement she was hovering above her in an attempt to pull her up into a hug.

Emily stood and allowed Kiami to wrap her arms around her. *I brought this on myself*, she thought as she peered over Kiami's shoulder at Justin. He was grinning from ear to ear, and as his eyes caught hers, he shot her a wink.

"At least now I don't feel so foolish about what happened in the woods," Emily breathed as she backed out of Kiami's embrace."

"I thought maybe you wouldn't be affected, like the jinn." Kiami's voice sounded peppier now, even when apologizing.

Emily furrowed her brow. "The jinn aren't affected? How do you know that?

"Well, until I met Aden I didn't, but..."

Both Emily and Justin spoke in unison. "Aden?"

Justin shot her a sharp look. "Kiami, explain."

"Everything I told you about Amanda was true. I just left Aden out of the story." Kiami's smile faltered, and she wrung her hands. "I'm embarrassed. I am sorry. I wasn't raised to behave like that."

Emily thought she looked like a deflated balloon as she made her way back to her seat.

Justin shook his head. "What a tangled mess. Just start by telling Emily what you told me."

"I had no idea what I was doing, I still don't. I'm just playing it by ear."

"As I explained to Justin earlier, it seemed harmless when I agreed. And I guess I was desperate to find someone like me." She looked back down at her lap, her voice fading almost to a whisper as she continued. "Now, I don't know what I think... I told Justin that she asked me to watch you, Emily. To spy on you a bit." She looked up into Emily's eyes. "She said that she had once encountered magic like mine, and she would take me to the wizard responsible if I helped her."

Emily crossed her arms over her chest. "Wizard?"

"Yes, but that's just what she wanted Aden to know ... she also asked me to find out why the jinni are here living in the Human realm." She threw an apologetic look at Justin. "You see, Emily, she knew things about you and me, only I had never met her before." She shook her head. "I don't believe I had ever met anyone that wasn't human before." She crinkled her nose.

"You mean like the jinni?" Emily asked.

"There are more races than just the jinni and the humans. I thought that maybe they had explained it to you at the party."

Emily thought of the strange creation myth that Gemma had recited at the diner right before she left. In the story they had mentioned several different types of magical beings and how they had all been separated into different realms. *It was just a kid's story...*

The tone of Justin's voice made Emily wince as he interrupted her thoughts, sounding irritated. "We would have, but the party was broken up a little earlier than expected because someone decided to fly through a window." He scowled at Kiami.

Kiami stood up quickly and spun to face him. "But that's just it ... I didn't fly through the window. I followed you to spy on the party, but I saw Aden go into the bookstore, and I followed him."

"So why bother following at all?" Emily interjected.

"You didn't meet Amanda. She was quite adamant that Aden not be involved. She had him drop me off far away from the town for a reason. She claims she's responsible for him because she freed him from some sorcerer's control."

Emily listened to Kiami's retelling of the events that brought Amanda and Aden together. With everything that had been going on, she had forgotten how Justin had also mentioned the word "realms" when they had been talking before.

As Kiami finished her explanation of the events that had occurred while Emily and Justin were at the party, Emily only felt more confused. "Why would they take him and lie about what happened, Justin?"

"I'm not sure, but if he's a jinni, as Kiami says, then no harm will come to him. They are probably just being cautious. First Emily, and now the two of you; it's more action than this sleepy town has ever seen."

Emily turned her gaze back to Kiami. "You said Amanda is not all human, that her mother came from a different realm. Does that mean you and I aren't human?

"I don't have those answers. That's part of the reason I agreed. I hoped that this wizard she talked about, Bloise, would be able to help me understand."

"That was quite an interesting story," Justin said, moving between them. "But how do we know you are still not keeping things from us?"

"I swear it's everything I know for sure. I think she means well... It's just a feeling, but I believe she may have been leaving some things out because she is still struggling to understand what has happened to her, what is still happening to her."

Justin crossed his arms over his chest. "So then we will just wait and see what happens. Gemma isn't going to keep everyone in the village in the dark."

Kiami glared at both of them. "You didn't meet Amanda. I have seen some of the things she has learned to do. If he doesn't show up soon, she may come looking for him."

"She learned to do?"

"Amanda has a whole library of spells and information. I think she prefers it to her own inherited powers. I got the feeling that she gets very uneasy about using her natural gifts."

Emily turned to Justin. "Maybe if we could find out where Aden is, we could talk him into helping us get to Amanda before she comes here looking?"

"Let's just see what Gemma and Zia have to say about all of this. Aden doesn't sound like someone we should be trying to help."

26

Amanda - A New Host

Amanda replayed that last nightmare in her head as she paced the library, waiting for any word from Aden. She knew that although it had only been a few days in the Arcane realm, as much as two weeks could very well have passed in the Human realm since he left with Kiami, and no matter what she did to distract herself, she couldn't shake the idea that something was wrong.

Then confirmation had come when she least expected it. She had been preparing herself by reading about shadow magic, a subject she had avoided as much as possible until now, when she fell into the short-lived vision.

At first she had thought it was all wrong; she could see both Kiami and Emily as plain as day, and then her view changed and she was staring into a fireplace.

Still, the host felt unfamiliar, and she could hear the girls talking from the other side of the room.

"She said that she had once encountered magic like mine, and she would take me to the wizard responsible if I helped her. *Kiami.*

"Wizard?" *Emily.*

She was seeing through yet another person's eyes. Worse were the feelings that were being transferred from her host: doubt, fear, betrayal, and confusion surrounded Amanda. This person was an emotional mess and was trying to hide it from Kiami and Emily.

"Yes, but that's just what she wanted Aden to know..." *Kiami.*

Then the conversation clouded as the emotions around her dulled. She could hear him, only he was not speaking out loud. The thought pushed at her hard like a punch to the chest. *Get out.* Somehow, he had known she was there. He had felt her presence, and he was fighting against her.

"I swear it's everything I know for sure. I think she means well..." *Kiami's muffled voice.*

Get out! screamed all around her, even louder, and she felt like she was reeling backward. She could already hear the sound of cascading water in her ears before the vision had fully cleared away.

Amanda sat there, stunned, rubbing the back of her sore head. Somehow the chair she had been sitting in had tipped, spilling her onto the floor.

There was no time to hesitate. She would have to wait to pick the vision apart. She had to move now. From the bits and pieces of the conversation she had heard, it was clear that her nightmare tormentor had been telling the truth, and what was worse, Kiami had brought Emily and someone else into it. She only hoped that Kiami hadn't revealed everything she had learned about her and her heritage.

She did her best to swallow her fear as she snatched up her powerful stone and Aden's dagger, preparing to return to the Human realm.

It seemed like the trails had been unused for some time, and Amanda marveled at the fact that the forest floor was overgrown with unkempt vegetation.

Tears prickled at her eyes as she reminded herself that in this realm, it had been years since she had walked this path with her father.

Once she was just deep enough in to see shadows cast at her feet, she pulled the gem from her pocket and clutched it tightly, pressing it into her palm.

The ground rumbled lightly beneath her as she attempted to command her own dark silhouette for the first time.

She watched unmoving as the misshapen shadow at her feet stretched outward slowly like a spilled bottle of ink. A few yards ahead, it veered off sharply to the right, and Amanda began to follow, concentrating all her attention on the shadow at her feet to stop herself from remembering.

When she got to the end of the inky trail and looked up into the tree's twisted branches, her knees felt weak. She pulled the familiar sheath from her boot and turned it over in her hand, admiring Jacob's twisted craftsmanship.

She tugged at the silver hilt, uncovering the stone dagger. Things would go faster if she used it to cut into the ground.

Amanda placed the dagger's sheath beside her and dug as quickly as she could. When she saw the top of a twisted tree root appear, she dropped the dagger and sheath into the hole and smoothed the dirt back over it.

Her heart pounded as she sat back on her heels. She breathed in deeply and exhaled slowly. A sharp cracking noise sounded above her. Amanda let out a startled yelp as a blur of brown movement entered her line of vision.

No more than an inch in front of her, a long, slender branch landed with a resounding thud. As Amanda bent forward to grab the gift, an icy chill ran up her arm, and she gasped. The ground around the tree was now covered in a shimmering layer of frost. Pink and white flowers blossomed all along its stubby branches, looking out of place.

She pushed herself up from the cold ground. Her eyes frantically darted around the woods; the scene was all too familiar. Half expecting a pair of green eyes to be watching her from a distance, Amanda gulped back tears. Her hands began to shake as she tried to hold her black diamond firmly at the staff's top, muttering the words she had practiced.

New growths sprouted up beneath Amanda's hand, forcing her to retract it and adjust her grip as they twisted around the gemstone, securing it in place.

27

Emily - Second Thoughts

As they filed out the door to meet Gemma at the bookstore, Emily felt Kiami grasp at her arm. Her palm was sweaty against Emily's skin, and despite the smile that was pasted on her face, her eyes were wide as she spoke.

"I'm going to stay behind, if you don't mind. Maybe check out the forest some more."

Emily's eyes darted from Kiami to Justin. "I can stay with her."

His shoulders dropped, and he raised a hand to sweep his hair back from his face. "No. I need you to go with me." He pointed to himself. "I have a reputation for being a joker, remember? And I don't think it's a good idea for either of you to go back in there. Let me ask around..."

Kiami interrupted, still clinging firmly on to Emily. "It's normal again."

Emily jerked her head toward the woods, scanning the property. The bright red petals that had been scattered across the yard were gone, and the forest's edge did appear less dense to her. "It seems okay to me." She shrugged. "If she feels safer here..."

Kiami's hand fell away from her arm as Justin spoke up. "It's just that they may want to hear from Kiami."

"I will go with you and help explain. It's not like Kiami is going to disappear or something."

Justin folded his arms over his chest. "Fine. Whatever. I am obviously outnumbered here, and standing around isn't going to help anything."

Emily stared out the car window at Kiami as she crept toward the forest's edge, taking a few small steps at a time and pausing to scan the ground.

"What do you think she is looking for?"

"Whatever it is, I hope she doesn't find it until we get back," Justin grunted. As the engine roared to life, Kiami turned back toward them and gave a quick wave with her hand.

Emily waved back as they moved down the path away from her. "All I know is she's less frightened of whatever is going on with the woods than she is of going back into town."

As they stood at the entrance to the bookstore, a chill ran through Emily, and she clutched her amethyst. She couldn't explain the sudden feeling of dread that filled her. She wasn't afraid to talk to Gemma and the others about Kiami and Aden. It was something else she couldn't quite place.

Emily looked up and down the road before following. Even though it was still early in the evening, several buildings had white and red signs hanging from the windows or doors announcing that they were closed for business.

Goosebumps formed on her arms, and she worked to rub them away. Despite the sun still being high, no one seemed to be out and about. The town was as quiet as the first night she had stepped into it.

She cleared her throat as Justin reached for the door. "Maybe we should go back and get Kiami."

Justin turned around with a jerk. "What?"

Wow, someone's grumpy, Emily thought as she raised her hands and took a step back. "Never mind. I'm sure I'm just being paranoid."

She heard him mutter, "Girls," as he spun back around and swung the door open.

28

Kiami - We Are All Monsters

Kiami didn't know what she had expected to find as she hunted the forest floor for clues, but Amanda hadn't been it.

Determined to find evidence of the experience, she had been focusing her attention on the ground, looking under leaves and rocks for anything, a tiny chunk of brightly colored moss or even an unidentifiable seed, as evidence of what had happened.

The relief she had felt when the car pulled away vanished. *I should have taken my chances in town,* she thought. She had been afraid to go back after the incident on the monument, and searching the forest seemed less dangerous.

Amanda stood only a few feet away, lingering in the gloom of the trees, shrouded by darkness. Shadowy figures seemed to surround her as she stared back in Kiami's direction, sneering.

"Had I known how badly you wanted to see my power, I would have given you a much better display at the castle." She balanced a wooden staff out in front of her, covering the top with her hand. "It seems no matter how hard I try, I just can't avoid the demon magic that runs through my veins. Did you tell them about that, Kiami?"

Kiami straightened herself and brought her arms to her sides, shaking her head in response. This was a different threat, and she needed to be careful how she engaged. "I am not your enemy."

"Keep your mouth shut." The earth trembled beneath her as Amanda spoke, causing her to stumble forward. The trees around her groaned and shook as she was forced to her knees by the earth's rippling movement.

Amanda lurched out and grabbed a handful of Kiami's hair, yanking her violently backward. Kiami's voice echoed through the forest as she screamed in agony. Her scalp stung as hair tore loose.

Kiami gritted her teeth and clenched her fists. The urge to change into owl form was almost too much to bear.

Amanda leaned over her and placed a finger at her lips. "Shhh."

Kiami found herself unable to speak or move as the shadows swarmed them both, engulfing her in darkness.

Kiami's scalp throbbed from the assault, and she tried to reach up to feel the damage, but her muscles still wouldn't obey her.

"Sorry about the uncomfortable travel arrangements, but without a jinn to transport us back into the castle, I had to seek out an alternate method. It's not an ideal form of travel, but hey, we are on a time crunch, and you already wasted so much of mine." Amanda's shoes made a click-clack noise against the hard stone floor as she moved around her.

Kiami tried to follow the sound of Amanda's voice with her eyes, but even they seemed to be in a state of paralysis, and she was stuck staring straight up at the dull gray ceiling.

"You are here for your own protection, whether you believe it or not." Amanda leaned over her and muttered what seemed to Kiami a few words that amounted to nothing more than gibberish. "There now, sit up."

As she pulled herself forward into a sitting position, Amanda thrust a cup under her nose. "Drink up." Kiami accepted the drink, watching Amanda over the brim as she swallowed the thick, tangy liquid. "That will keep you from singing me any lullabies."

Kiami's throat tingled when she opened her mouth to speak. "I believe that you think what you're doing is necessary." Her voice crackled with the effort. "I don't know why Aden went to town. It had nothing to do with me."

Amanda lowered her eyes and shook her head slowly back and forth. "You just couldn't do what you were asked." She poked at Kiami's chest with her finger. "You have exacerbated my problem by bringing Emily directly into this. There was still a chance she could have been safe until you interfered. Or at the very least she could have died blissfully unaware. Free of the burden that I have had to endure."

Kiami leaned forward and rubbed her temples. "I want to understand, Amanda, I do. But you're telling me nothing."

"Selfish. You didn't NEED to know. It was safer for you not to know." Amanda resumed pacing the room. "Everything you do has an effect. EVERYTHING!"

That's it. Kiami slapped her hand down onto the floor and

pushed herself up into a standing position to face Amanda. She took a quick, graceful step forward and raised her hand, striking Amanda across the face as hard as she could with her palm. "YOU ARE BEING CRAZY!"

She watched unmoving as Amanda placed her hands above her knees and bent forward, breathing in deeply and counting each breath as she slowly exhaled.

She had counted to eleven before she raised her head back up to meet Kiami's gaze. "Thank you."

"Were you having a panic attack?"

Amanda raised her hand as if to wave the question away. "Don't worry, they will come for you, I am sure, and one by one I will snatch them up and tuck them all away in the safety of the castle. It's the only way for now until I figure this out."

"You can't just keep us here."

Amanda's mouth stretched into a wide smile. "I like you, Kiami. You are braver than I thought. But keep in mind that I will do whatever it takes to set things right."

"But I don't understand."

"Listen, Kiami, don't try to play innocent with me. I was there when you kissed the boy on the beach, and I saw exactly what happened to him."

Kiami's eyes widened as she backed away. "You were there?"

"Reminds you that good and evil aren't always as cut-and-dry as they seem, doesn't it?"

"I didn't mean to."

"Does that really make a difference?"

Kiami folded her arms across her chest and looked away as she whispered, "I'm some kind of monster."

"Yes, well, keep your chin up. We are all monsters."

In stunned silence, she watched as Amanda spun on her heels

and headed for the doorway. Just as she reached the first step, she turned her head back. "I think it will be best if you stay down here until everybody shows up."

As the last stone shifted into place, concealing the doorway, Kiami collapsed onto the small bed. The terrible memory of the day she met the boy on the beach was fresh in her mind.

Kiami had slept restlessly the night before, nervous for what the morning wouldn't bring on the anniversary of the day she had come into Rhiannon and Jacqueline's care. The day that they had always celebrated as her birthday.

Jacqueline had retreated to her room early the night before, as she had most evenings since Rhiannon's death. Things had already been going on that way for weeks, and Kiami held out little hope of Jacqueline acknowledging the occasion.

The sky was still dim when she rolled out of bed, and Kiami had decided she would make the most of the day by greeting the morning sun as it rose up beyond the deep blue sea. Walks on the shore had always brought her comfort, and she had known that the beach would likely be deserted at this early hour.

Morning was the most tranquil time on the beach, and to her it seemed a shame that more people didn't stop to notice the way the sun emerged above the edge of the sky, sending out wispy pink and red streaks as if it was trying to embrace the world with those tendrils.

Kiami raised her hand to her chest in surprise as she turned to leave her room. A small, wrapped package sat on her dresser. She almost screamed with excitement, despite the early morning hour.

It wasn't the gift that filled her with happiness, but the thought behind it, proof that Jacqueline still loved her like a daughter.

Inside she found a beautiful transparent stone. When she held it up to the light, it seemed to shimmer a silvery blue from within. Kiami was taken aback by its phenomenal beauty, and she quickly made a plan to harness the gemstone so she would be able to wear it as a necklace. She dumped her box of craft supplies onto the floor and sifted through the contents, looking for leftover gold wiring. When she found the small coil, she wrapped it around the gem several times as tightly as she could.

When she was sure the gem was secure, she created a loop and twisted it at the bottom so that she could slip one of her small chains through the opening and fasten it around her neck. Kiami had accomplished the task within minutes. She couldn't stop smiling as she admired her gift and her handiwork in the mirror, turning the gem around in her fingers.

Since it was still too early to wake Jacqueline to thank her for the treasure, she resumed with her original plan.

She made her way down to the beach just as the sun began to peek over the horizon. The sea lapped gently against the shore as she walked, relishing the feeling of the grainy sand beneath her feet and between her toes. In her state of bliss, she had forgotten herself and began to hum a song as she moved closer to the shoreline, where the water drenched the sand.

Someone else's footprints were molded into her intended path, and she followed them, still humming as she moved.

By the time she spotted him and the fact that she wasn't alone sank in, it was too late.

He stared at her and away from the sea, a flat stone clutched tightly in his hand, forgotten. His eyes were wild. His sandy brown hair was windblown. He seemed to stand a full foot taller than her, and at that moment Kiami thought he looked even more magical than the sunrise she had ventured out to see.

She crept closer until she was within inches of him, and although she had made the conscious effort to stifle her song, he did not speak. Instead, he leaned down and began to wrap his arms around her. Kiami accepted the comfort of his embrace and returned it as he boldly moved in to plant a quick kiss on her lips.

It was her first kiss, and she closed her eyes in anticipation of the warm, fuzzy feelings she had heard described in books. But instead, his arms went lank beside her, and as she opened her eyes, he gasped as if he was in pain.

Kiami tried to let go, but she had found herself incapable of freeing him from her grasp. Unable to detach himself, he stood upright but remained unmoving against her, and she was forced to watch his face in horror as his smooth skin wrinkled and took on a leathery texture. He seemed to be aging in front of her eyes, as if she had literally sucked the life from him.

A shrill scream escaped her throat as he finally slipped through her arms, landing at her feet. His once bright eyes were now dull and gray, staring up at her, unblinking. As her own eyes filled with tears, she collapsed beside his still deteriorating form.

Nothing like this had ever happened when she sang before. She tucked her knees up to her chest and gazed through her tears at the skeletal remains beside her.

Her wailing cries, she thought, were what had brought Jacqueline down from the house. By the time Kiami noticed her hovering above her, the remains were no more than dust.

Jacqueline's mouth had been set in a grim line. Something burned in her eyes, fear or anger, Kiami hadn't been sure. As she pushed herself up onto her feet, she knew there would be no comforting words offered.

Kiami flipped over onto her back and wiped her tear-soaked face. The springs in the flimsy mattress squeaked beneath her.

Resolute that she had made the right decision in allowing Amanda to bring her here, she would wait patiently for her new friends to arrive.

29

Emily - The Jinn's Request

The secret space below the bookstore was no ordinary basement, and Emily couldn't help but wonder if she hadn't been transported to someplace else entirely as she passed through the wooden door.

Instead of a staircase on the other side, as she was expecting, there was a winding tunnel that sloped downward as she progressed. She marveled at the odd construction, but stranger still was the fact that the light filling the tunnel had no noticeable source.

She followed close behind Gemma as she crossed through a rounded stone doorway and into a large room. The intense smell of mothballs and incense tickled at her nose, causing a sneezing fit.

When she regained control of herself, she opened her eyes to see an unfamiliar young man standing in front of her. *This has to be Aden,* she reasoned as she rubbed at the bridge of her nose, trying to sooth her irritated nasal passages.

She dropped her hand back to her side and stared at the intruder. Dark hair hung around his face. His startling green eyes seemed somehow ageless. His lips were set in a thin line as he looked fixedly back at her, and Emily couldn't help but feel as if he was sizing her up for a fight.

A gentle nudging hand on her shoulder pulled her out of his gaze.

"I hope you understand, Emily, we were hesitant to bring either of you into this."

She spun around and threw a half smile at Gemma.

"Asad had gone missing, and we had to wonder if he had a part in his disappearance." She added gesturing to Aden, "At least we know it wasn't him, although we haven't ruled out his companion."

"Kiami?"

Gemma clicked her tongue. "Heavens no, that Amanda girl ... she is right to think we are the keepers of secrets. But to not trust us for it... And we agree with Aden. He does need to be getting back to her. We have high hopes that he can guide her in the right direction."

She raised her eyebrows and smiled awkwardly back at Emily. "With yours and Justin's help, of course."

Emily glanced over at Justin and wasn't surprised to see him offer Gemma only a shrug in response before leaning nonchalantly back against the wall.

She turned her eyes back to Gemma and grabbed her hand. "I will do whatever I can."

Gemma gave her fingers a light squeeze before releasing them. "The fact is I need both of you on board with Aden. Foremost, Amanda trusts him. But there is more to it than that." She dropped her smile and turned to Justin. "Stop pouting and come away from the wall."

Emily bit at her lip to hold back a grin. He hadn't known about the lower level of the bookstore, and the secret seemed to irritate him to no end.

"Now, where should we start? I need to word this very carefully..." Gemma glanced back and forth between them. "The fact is, we wish we could share our knowledge with the world, but we can't." She looked up at Aden and gestured for him to join them before continuing,

"Being the only race to keep a true written account of the time before the realms, we were sworn to secrecy. The jinn are only allowed to pass the knowledge down to other jinni. We have shared this knowledge with Aden to help him with the mission Amanda is on."

She turned to Justin and gave him a tight hug. "You will always be one of us, and we love you dearly, but you are half human, and so we cannot share that history with you."

Emily spoke as she moved to stand beside Justin and drape her arm over his shoulder. "I think I understand, Gemma. You are physically unable to speak about it?"

She nodded. "Justin, you have grown up with us. Aden has not lived amongst jinn since he was very young. You can help him." She gave him a playful poke at the chest.

Emily smiled as Justin finally looked up to meet Gemma's eyes, and she grinned at him before turning to address the room.

"Know that within every myth there lies a speck of truth. But you must open your eyes to see it ... and you may not want to." Gemma clapped her hands.

"When the myth of the world was created, the jinn did it in conjunction with the goddesses, or rather our race agreed with them and entered into a binding contract of sorts..." She gestured to the walls. "This is an illustrated version of the events we agreed to pass on."

Emily noticed for the first time that the stone walls held

colorful images. At first glance, the picture to her right looked like an explosion of twinkling yellow dots in a dark empty space, but as she recalled the start of the myth from the party and took a better look, she could see the suggested outline of two humanoid forms.

She reached out to the rough wall and let her fingers glide over the paint, studying the image of the celestial beings. *If every myth holds a speck of truth, maybe I can discover secrets about myself here.*

She moved slowly to the next picture, trying to memorize the shapes and colors. The story itself was no longer fresh in her mind, but pieces resurfaced as she witnessed the growth of the triplets from babies to children and then to young women being sent out to create worlds of their own.

The others continued to talk from somewhere in the room, but their voices were no more than muffled static in her ears as she progressed, drawn toward the final two images. Her movement stopped as her fingertips brushed against the illustration of the gifts.

All three goddesses were crudely outlined in it, and yet Emily felt like it held more detail than any of the others, and she wondered if it had been painted by the same person.

Akila appeared to be kneeling and digging in the earth with one hand. A seed rested in the open palm of the other, ready to be buried beneath the soil. Mia stood beside her, both of her outstretched hands were filled with gemstones, each a different color. The third sister, Sophia, seemed to hover in front of the other two, her face shrouded by the hood of a cloak draped over her form.

The hair on the back of Emily's neck prickled, and she reached into her pocket to grab her amethyst before forcing herself toward the last image. Here, three gnarled trees lined each side of a dirt road, with one final tree resting in the center of the path in the distance.

Emily chewed at her lip. This image didn't appear to be directly related to the rest, and it didn't seem to have anything to do with what she remembered from the myth. She took a step back and noticed that each tree was distinctly different. One was covered in red-petaled flowers and surrounded by tall vegetation, while the tree next to it was covered in a blanket of snow.

"Gemma said that those trees represent the different realms."

Emily jumped at the sound of the unfamiliar voice and spun around to see Aden had moved beside her. She gave a quick nod and turned back toward the painting before reaching her arm up to point at the gray tree that was blocking the path. "So what's this one's realm?"

Aden shrugged. "You will have to go back into the bookstore and ask Gemma."

Emily glanced around her; she hadn't noticed that they were the only two remaining in the basement.

"We should get moving before they notice we aren't behind them."

Emily nodded. She took one last fleeting look at the painting before heading quickly up the passage behind Aden.

Justin was waiting for her at the top with his arms folded in front of him. "What were you doing down there? I don't trust that guy."

"I guess I was off in my own little world. Probably would have stayed there all day if Aden hadn't told me you left." She cocked an eyebrow at him. "Where's Gemma?"

"Really, Em, you're messing with me, right?"

Emily shook her head.

"So you expect me to believe that you didn't hear Cherry come and tell her that Mrs. Nazari needed her?" Justin stared back at her, unbelieving.

"I didn't hear, sorry."

"Something attacked her in the woods."

Emily's eyes went wide. "We have to get back to Kiami."

Justin scowled as Aden stepped beside her and placed his hand on her shoulder. "It wasn't Amanda. Cherry said it was an old man that attacked Mrs. Nazari."

Justin threw his hands up. "What if she was in disguise?"

Aden lifted his hand from her shoulder and took a step closer to Justin. "He didn't even use magic."

"That was the story Cherry told us, but how are we supposed to know if it wasn't just another cover for something worse?"

Emily shook her head in disbelief. "Stop, just stop, both of you." She took a deep breath and pushed past them toward the door. "We need to go. Now."

It did not appear that Kiami had returned to the house while they were in town, and Emily's heart sank.

Justin had maintained his standoffish attitude with Aden for the entire ride, and she was hoping once Kiami was with them, he would return to his usual self.

"I'm going to go look for her in the woods. Aden, come with me." Emily motioned for him to follow as she reached for the door handle.

"Don't go anywhere alone with him." Justin grabbed at her shoulder, bringing her to a halt halfway through the door. "Besides, what if it changes again?"

With all they had learned, they forgot to mention the weird changes in the forest to Gemma. Emily glanced between them both and bit her lip to stop herself from grinning. Their faces held the same worried expression. *They are both being so stubborn.*

Emily wondered if they even realized how similar they were. Aden was just trying to protect Amanda, the same way Justin was trying to protect her.

"Fine, we will all go, together."

"No." Justin shook his head. "What if she comes back? Maybe she's just where we can't see her. We will go, you stay."

Emily crossed her arms and smirked at the pair. "How will you look for her if you won't even look at each other?"

Justin rubbed at the back of his neck and grunted.

"Both of you," she added, raising her eyebrows.

Aden thrust his hand out in Justin's direction. "Sorry."

"Em," Justin groaned.

"You promised Gemma."

Justin grabbed at Aden's hand and gave it a fast shake. "Sorry."

Emily watched from the window as the pair crossed the yard and moved into the forest. Once they were out of sight, she pulled a chair out from under the table and took a seat. She was pretty sure they would not find Kiami in the forest. The feeling of dread that had overtaken her outside of the bookshop had never really cleared up completely.

It lingered, tugging at her, much like the way she had felt the need to keep moving when she had left home. She didn't know where the feeling came from, but she just knew Kiami was not perfectly fine. She cradled her head in her arms on the tabletop.

I shouldn't have let her stay behind.

As strong as the urge was to get to Kiami, she would have to wait for them to return from the woods.

She laid her head down into her arms, reminding herself that Kiami wasn't exactly helpless. She tried to imagine what it would take to keep a person that could both shapeshift and control people with their voice restrained. The idea seemed impossible to her, but then she was unfamiliar with this world of magic. She felt like she could fit everything she knew about it in the palm of one hand. Maybe nothing was impossible.

Emily lifted her head as the muted sound of voices came from the garage. Eager to find out why they were back so quickly, she hurried to the door just as Justin pushed it open.

She spoke quickly as she wrung her hands. "That was fast. What's happened?"

Justin glanced back at Aden, motioning for him to enter the house. "We found something in the woods."

Emily took a step back to let them enter. "Well, what is it?"

Justin brushed his hair back from his face and let out a sigh. "Go on, show her, Aden."

Aden stepped closer to Emily and held up a large wad of hair. Emily moved in to get a better look at the mess. Amid the thick black locks, several silver strands shimmered. She closed her eyes and gulped. There was no doubt it was Kiami's.

"Em, there was something else. The ground looked wrong where we found it. Not in the way it had before. It looked like it was coming apart." He looked up at Aden, who was still clutching the hair in his fist. "You explain it ... and please throw that away, it's kind of grossing me out."

Aden dropped the wad of hair into the garbage bin and turned back to Emily. "When Amanda uses her natural shadow magic, it has a destructive effect on everything around her." He paused a moment and looked back over his shoulder at the place he had thrown the hair. "Although this anomaly on the ground seemed to be concentrated on a particular area, the outcome was very similar. I think maybe it's proof that she came and took Kiami."

Emily put her hand on her hip. "How could she just take her? I haven't known Kiami long, but I know she is not helpless."

"Yes, well neither is Amanda. And apparently Aden failed to mention something to Gemma. Right, Aden?"

Anger flashed across Aden's face as he looked at Justin. "She did what she had to do. But yes, she freed a jinni in the past."

Emily motioned with her hand for him to stop. "We have all

made mistakes. Well, maybe not you, Justin, you haven't had to make any hard choices, and I am glad, but you have to understand. This is not something we can walk away from. You didn't judge me this way when I showed up in town."

"Emily, you didn't threaten people and kidnap them. And when he says freed, he means to say she stabbed him..."

"Enough. I don't think it's wise for you or any of us to go into this thing with our minds already made up about her. We are supposed to be helping Aden get her on the right path. Gemma would not have asked us if it wasn't important."

"But it wasn't in self-defense, Em."

"Justin, stop! Aden, how certain are you that Amanda is the one that took her?"

"I am fairly certain. Almost positive."

"Well then, we need to go."

Aden spoke up again. "Justin said he isn't able to travel through realms without help, and I haven't ever tried to bring two humans to another realm on my own."

"Well, it's a good thing both of us are not entirely human then." Emily crossed her arms and shot him a nervous smile. "Let's just give it a shot, shall we?"

30

Emily - On Shaky Ground

Darkness had begun to fall as Emily readied herself for travel to the Arcane realm. Aden had warned them that with two passengers, the trip would not be as smooth as usual. She had shrugged it off. Since she had never traveled with a jinni before, she wouldn't have anything to compare it to.

Standing on Aden's right, she wrapped her arm around his waist. Justin mirrored her from Aden's left. A gust kicked up around them almost immediately.

In this strange semi-huddle, Aden stepped forward into the wind. Emily did her best to imitate his movement. She was lifted, walking through the air, and she understood why he had termed it "traveling with the wind."

Aden shouted through the cyclone around them, "You probably shouldn't look down. This is likely to be a bumpy ride. Don't let go."

The vortex changed direction quickly, and the world below them seemed to shift and melt away.

Emily struggled to regain her hold as her arm slipped slightly down Aden's back. For a split second, she felt as if she was falling. She flailed her free arm around, grasping aimlessly. It was just long enough for her stomach to leap up into her throat before she felt Justin's hand grasp her free arm from the other side.

Emily squeezed her eyes shut, waiting for the voyage to end.

They stumbled forward as they touched the ground. She dropped her hands and bent over on her knees, trying to find her bearings as the ground tilted unnaturally, rolling outward like a wave.

Once the vertigo subsided, Emily slowly turned in a circle. A field stretched out around them. In one direction she could make out a line of trees far off in the distance. Closer to her left, a pond shimmered in what seemed to be the midday sun. The earth beneath her tilted again, and she lifted her arms, trying to steady herself.

"Em, are you all right?" Justin reached out and grabbed her arm.

"I'm fine, just a little unbalanced."

"Why don't you sit down for a few minutes?"

She nodded as she lowered herself to the ground before looking up at her travel companions. Aden and Justin seemed unfazed by the trip; in fact, Justin looked happier to her than he had since this whole thing started. He grinned foolishly as he took in their surroundings.

Aden kneeled down beside her. "I don't suppose you're ready to go for another trip?"

Emily shook her head.

"It will be necessary when you two get to the castle. You guys can walk from here if you prefer."

"Aren't you coming with us?"

"I want to go on ahead and have a word with Amanda. I will meet you outside when you arrive. It won't take you long to walk. But Emily, I will have to help you inside. There are no visible entrances or exits, and the few larger windows were spelled long ago so that although you can see out of them, nothing can pass through."

"You are abandoning us?" Justin bellowed from behind her.

"You should be safe. Don't worry, it's straight ahead. If you lose your bearings, just keep going toward the sound of water."

Emily made a shooing motion. "Go, we will be fine."

Aden gave her a fast nod before moving away. She watched as the blades of grass and flowers around his feet bent and swayed as if pulled by a cyclone of wind she couldn't see, and within moments he was carried out of her view.

As Emily lay back onto the ground, grass tickled at her bare skin. "I just need a few more minutes."

Justin leaned down, grinning again. "I suppose I should be flattered that you trust I can take care of you in an unfamiliar land."

Emily couldn't help but smile at his remark; she missed his normal playful attitude. "Quiet, you!" She gave a halfhearted swat in his direction. Something tickled at her arm, and she swatted again. "Stop it."

"Stop what?"

The sensation grew. "Ugh." She swatted again.

Where her hand met her flesh, a burning sensation erupted. She sat forward and looked at the area of the attack. There was no red blemish or small bump. She didn't see anything, but still, the burning continued and seemed to be spreading up toward her shoulder. Emily stood and rubbed at her arm just as something tickled at her leg. She swatted at the new irritation, and again her skin burned as her hand landed on her leg.

Justin gripped her hand and tugged. Emily had not noticed him watching as she batted at the unseen assailant. "Em?"

"It burns, everywhere," she managed to stammer, as she continued to swat at the invisible irritant while also trying to ignore the places where the crawling sensation had only just begun. "Is it some bug or something?" She grunted. "Do you see anything at all?"

He yanked her hard, pulling her toward him. "I don't see anything."

"Then what are you doing?"

"Going to the pond."

Hoping that it would at least lessen the sensation, Emily half ran, half stumbled as he jerked her toward the water, still clutching her hand.

He didn't hesitate as he pulled her into the clear water, still fully clothed, and Emily couldn't help but laugh at the situation. The discomfort on her leg faded on contact. *Maybe I am allergic to something in the grass,* she thought.

Relieved, she waded forward until the liquid reached her shoulders before ducking her head underneath. She didn't want to take a chance that any of the irritants could be left behind.

When she resurfaced, Justin's back was turned to her. He had only gone into the pond up to his waist, so the upper half of his clothing had remained dry. Seizing the opportunity, she flattened her hand and splashed water at him, soaking the back of his shirt.

Instead of turning around and returning the attack, Justin raised a finger in the air and motioned for her to join him.

He was watching something in the pond.

Emily moved around the side of him. A small, pale-green creature floated on top of the water directly in front of them. She watched as Justin reached his arm out in its direction. "Justin, I don't..."

"Shhh, you will scare it." At the sound of their voices, it lifted its head and cocked it to the side. Three small, twisted horns jutted up from behind its large, round eyes. The creature seemed to be about six inches long.

It began to paddle toward them with its four slender appendages. Its skin appeared slick and streamlined as it moved through the water. It stopped just at Justin's fingertips and turned its gilled face up at him.

Justin started to coo at the creature like it was a pet, and Emily shook her head in disapproval.

As the creature began to pull itself out of the water and into his hand, Emily could see that each appendage had three long, suction-cupped fingers.

"It's cute, right, Em?" he whispered. The creature began to inch up his arm.

"Sure, now put it back in the water. We have no idea what types of animals live here."

"Fine," Justin said, sounding defeated. But as he reached for the aquatic animal, it spread its appendages out, latching onto his bicep with its suction-cupped limbs. He gave it a gentle tug. "It won't come off."

Emily rolled her eyes and tugged at his arm. "Get out of the water." She could hear Justin mumbling under his breath as he followed her to the shore. "One second." She reached up and pulled her hair together in the shape of a tight ponytail then twisted hard in order to get some of the moisture out of it.

"I got this."

Emily's eyes went wide as she watched him lift his creature free arm high above his head. A large rock was clenched in his hand. She shrieked as she reached out to stop him. "You will kill that creature and hurt yourself in the process."

"You got a better idea?"

"Maybe. Can you make a flame?"

"Burn it off..."

"No." Emily shook her head in disgust. "He lives in the water, right? So, it's safe to say he probably needs to stay wet to some degree. Just make a fire and hold it near enough to dry him out a bit."

"I can try. Due to my half breed status — should I refer to myself like that? I never have before..." He looked up into Emily's eyes, the creature momentarily forgotten. "I guess I always just felt like I was the same as the other jinn, even though I wasn't."

"That's because you are, Justin. They are your family. Be thankful that you have them."

"I am, but..."

Emily cleared her throat and pointed to his arm. "You can try?"

"It's much more impressive when I control a flame that is already going strong."

"Well, you don't need to impress me. You just need to get that little thing off your arm." Emily placed her hand on her hip. "Besides, we only want a small flame anyway."

"Okay. But don't watch, you make me nervous."

"You can vanish into thin air and control hot fire without getting burned, but I make you nervous?"

"Sometimes."

Emily spun around so that her back was facing Justin. "Better?"

"Much."

She counted to sixty and then peeked over her shoulder. Justin had his hand spread open, his palm barely concealed in the orange wave of fire. She continued to watch as he lifted it toward the creature, keeping it only a few inches from its slimy body.

Her neck was starting to ache, and she snapped her head

forward just as she heard a tiny splash from behind her. She clapped her hands and spun around. "It worked?" Her eyes moved up Justin's arm. Small red dots were present where the creature had suction-cupped to his bare bicep. "Does that hurt?"

Justin shook his head. "We should get moving."

31

Amanda - Brewing Storm

The first thing Amanda noticed was that everything in the dream place looked wrong.

The tree branches were empty. A dozen golden colored apples lay squashed below its trunk. Their sweet smell hung in the air above them. Amanda bent down to inspect the pulpy mess before turning to look out into the field.

The stems of the wildflowers were bare. Their petals had been torn and shredded. The remnants lay scattered and muddied in the grass, as if the fiercest of storms had just blown through.

The gray sky crackled with electricity as she turned to Aden.

"Amanda." He was standing tall, but she thought she could hear a slight quiver in his voice.

"They've poisoned you against me."

Aden brushed a stray hair out of her face. "No. I am afraid for you, Amanda."

He reached for her again, and she pulled out of his reach. She noticed the way his back stiffened and tensed as she circled him.

"Why don't you try something? Fight me. Isn't that why you brought me here to the dream place?"

"I chose this place because I thought it would be safer for both of us to talk one on one." His eyes locked on to hers. "They didn't send me to fight you. They sent me, all of us, to help you."

Amanda looked away. "Even if you're telling the truth, the jinni from the tomb said we were ripping the world apart. She said I caused it."

His words were barely above a whisper. "Her poor choice of words is regrettable, but it's probably the only thing she could come up with to say." He reached forward and placed his hand on her shoulder. "I can see through your walls, Amanda. I know you don't want to hurt anyone."

She crossed her arms over her chest and took a deep breath. "Everything is a mess because of me. Maybe you don't know me as well as you think."

"The jinn in town showed me things. I want to explain more, but it's difficult."

Amanda heard hesitation in his words. Like the jinni Jacqueline, he stumbled in his speech, as if putting great thought into each syllable that left his mouth.

"Something's coming. It might even be here already. You need to know that they accept you for what you are. You don't have to face it alone. None of you do."

Amanda looked back up. "None of us?"

Aden opened his mouth to speak and then clamped it shut. His eyes went wide as an arm appeared below his chin, crossing over his chest.

Seeing Abaddon outside of her own nightmares for the first time was startling, and Amanda found herself backing away from the sight. The sound of his gravelly voice sent a shiver down her spine.

"What's the matter, little jinn, tongue-tied?" The monster behind Aden let out an inhuman snarl, exposing his pointed yellow teeth. "And you..." He shot a look of disgust at Amanda. "You can't do anything right."

Aden made no move to pull out of her nighttime tormentor's grasp as Abaddon spoke again.

He can't change form, or he would turn into smoke and vanish. Maybe this is what Erol meant when he said that the dream place could be even more dangerous. He said...

"All you had to do was kill one of them. Now I will give you one last choice, Amanda. Kill yourself or he dies."

...things work differently here.

"No, Amanda you don't have..." Aden's eyes bulged as her monster squeezed his chest.

A tear trickled down her cheek. "Please, stop." She dropped her arms to her sides. "Please."

His grin spread up beyond his earlobes, and Aden gasped for breath as he relaxed his grip.

"Good girl, go fetch the dagger you buried."

Aden pushed forward suddenly, shouting, "No, they all need you! I'm disposable."

Amanda couldn't hold back her tears any longer as she shouted back, "No you're not!"

The monster wrapped his other arm around Aden and covered his mouth with a blistered hand. "I could pull your head right off, little jinni. Remember that."

She wiped her face with her hand and turned toward the tree. "I caused this, Aden. I should pay. You have already been punished enough." She bent down and began to dig into the cold dirt with her fingers, searching for the blade.

The monster cackled from behind her as she reached the dagger and brought it up from the hole. Lightning flashed above them, causing the enchanted metal to glimmer in her hand.

Maybe if I am fast enough, I can get to him before he can hurt Aden. She lifted the dagger in her hand. The monster spoke as she stepped forward.

"Even if you succeeded in what you're thinking, you would only prolong the inevitable. And he will be dead long before you can pierce me with that blade." The monster gave his tongue a loud click. "It would be pointless for you to return without him. Wouldn't it, Aden?"

Amanda lowered the blade to her side and searched Aden's eyes.

"He told them, you know, about the jinni from your past, Erol." He let the name roll slowly off his tongue. "They will never believe that you didn't dispose of Aden the same way. They will never TRUST you."

She hesitated momentarily, as if contemplating what he was suggesting. *No.* She shook her head. They would never be able to accept her after the things she had done.

Without her crystal or her staff, she didn't see much of a choice. She clutched the dagger's handle in both her hands and pointed it toward her abdomen as the memory of how she freed Erol played in her mind. She had known that they were connected and that he could feel her emotions. She had expected him to fight back, wanted him to, but he hadn't. And after he had just disappeared like he had never been there to begin with...

Amanda wondered how much the monster actually knew about the jinn. She knew that when he killed Aden, the jinn's body would vanish almost instantly, leaving the monster open for attack. "I can't make that type of choice again," she whispered to herself.

The monster relaxed his brow and grinned. "You're tired of fighting, Amanda, aren't you? Our world is about to become a pretty scary place, and you have already had to go through so much."

She looked up into Aden's eyes, and he began to squirm and kick with all his strength as she mouthed the word "sorry." She sucked in a deep breath, still watching Aden struggle as she mentally prepared to pierce herself with the blade.

The monster's hand slipped just low enough for Aden to chomp down on it. Green blood oozed down his chin as he shouted, "You won't have to choose this time, Amanda. I am choosing for you. They need you. Show them who you really are!"

Abaddon's face twisted into a snarl as the monster wrapped his arm back around Aden's head. *He's going to kill him.*

Amanda let out a bloodcurdling scream and did the only thing she could do. She couldn't let Aden sacrifice himself for no reason. She turned the blade outward and concentrated on moving toward Abaddon with all her strength. She heard a grotesque cracking noise as the monster twisted Aden in its hands just as she slammed into him with all of her weight, howling in rage as she forced the dagger deeper into the monster's flesh.

Stealthily, she moved behind him while he was still in shock. No sound escaped his lips as she slid the blade into his back. Abaddon didn't disappear instantly, like Aden had. Instead, the image of him began to fade and become washed out. Lightning cracked across the sky, illuminating his hunched form as Amanda backed away with the dagger still clutched in her fist, shaking her head as she moved.

"What have you done, Aden? You have sacrificed yourself for nothing."

Another lightning strike thundered in her ears. They were becoming more frequent with each passing second, and she couldn't help but wonder how long it would take before she would be pulled from the dream world.

She fell to her knees at the site of the hole she had dug and dropped the slime-covered dagger back into it. Her hands trembled as she thought of Abaddon's words. *Our world is about to become a pretty scary place.* The sky rumbled and cracked again. Stinging hail began to pelt her skin as she pushed the dirt into place over the hole and leaned her back against the tree.

"It looks like the storm has just begun." *And I have no idea how to stop it.*

32

Best-Laid Plans...

Afraid to sit down in the grass again, Emily stood waiting, the sound of rushing water drowning out her thoughts. "How much longer, do you think?"

Justin shrugged. He seemed to be very interested in the castle; he had barely taken his eyes off it since they had arrived.

Eager to get this over with and return to town, Emily tapped her foot impatiently. The constant drone of the water was starting to get on her nerves. As she was yelling over the noise to get Justin's attention, it occurred to her that bad luck followed close behind whenever she was away from the place.

Emily twisted a lock of her hair between her fingers and looked up at the ledges, where the water began to spray down.

"Em, something's coming toward us, and I don't think it's Aden."

She spun on her heels to see what he was talking about. "What now?"

"Look there." He pointed around the side of the castle, where Emily could barely make out two blue lights bobbing up and down.

She released a relieved sigh and began to walk in the direction of the wisps.

Justin released a loud gasp from behind her. "What in the world are you doing?"

Plodding ahead, she ignored his question, and soon the wisps were circling her. She grinned back at Justin, who stood watching them with his mouth half open.

The wisps circled her again and moved a few feet back in the direction they had come from before stopping. "Come on, Justin."

He raised one of his eyebrows and crossed his arms. "You want to follow them now?"

Emily gave him an exaggerated shrug before explaining. "It's been my experience that if they want you to go somewhere, there's a good reason for it."

Justin dropped his arms back to his sides. "You know what these things are?"

"I call them wisps. They are the creatures that led me to town to begin with. Now come on, let's see what they want to show us."

Now that both of them were following, the wisps moved quickly along the side of the stone wall. Water splashed at Emily from all directions, and her clothes were soon soaked again.

They came to a halt at the back corner of the castle, where it met with the mountain cave's edge.

Restless, Kiami had circled the room multiple times, waiting for something to happen. Each time she returned to lie on the bed, her thoughts wandered back to Jacqueline and the last time she had seen her.

She swore something about the place, the sound of dripping water, or perhaps it was a scent in the air, something unseen, jogged the memory inside her. She just couldn't pinpoint the culprit.

She missed the complex aroma of the seaside and wondered if it was possible to duplicate the recipe, a pinch of salt and a dash of sulfur, sprinkled with a briny finish. Unlike the seashore, the air in the castle dungeon tasted stale.

How had everything gone so wrong that day? Kiami retraced her steps again. She had left her room in a complete state of bliss. She had left the shore in utter turmoil. Jacqueline had not just refused to comfort her — she had attacked as Kiami had lifted herself from the sand to embrace her.

She had missed something. Was there fear in Jacqueline's eyes as she had swatted Kiami's open arms away? Kiami had been too grief-stricken even to realize she was being rejected, and an odd struggle had ensued.

She hadn't felt the chain snap on her gift. She hadn't even

realized it was gone until several lonely tear-filled days had passed.

Trivial. Wishing she still had the necklace seemed wrong after everything that had happened to lead her here. *Maybe Amanda was right to call me selfish.*

Kiami rose from the mattress and dried her face, ready to make another trek around the stone room.

As she reached down to smooth out the fabric of her dress, a blue wispy ball darted at her, startling her. She froze and stared straight into the swirling orb.

In the forest, Emily and Amanda both seemed to be acquainted with these creatures, and neither had been upset by their presence. "Hello?" she whispered.

The wisp made a fast circle around her and then moved away from her toward the far corner. Kiami took a step forward, and the wisp moved again, almost touching the stones.

The wall glistened in the wisp's blue light, and Kiami reached forward to feel the damp water that trickled down it. Unsure of what the wisp wanted, Kiami bent down to inspect the few broken rock fragments that lay at her feet. The wisp followed her movement and then began to zigzag in front of her.

Kiami righted herself and shrugged at the blue ball. "I don't know what you want."

With one sudden movement, the wisp shot up along the wall's seam and then vanished.

"Hey!" She turned her face up to the ceiling and yelled, "Why did you do that?"

"Kiami?" The voice was muffled by the stones between them, but she easily recognized it as Emily's.

She pressed herself up against the wall and looked up. A jagged crack ran about three feet along the ceiling, where the water was coming in. The rocks had begun to separate and crumble just enough to leave a gap a few inches wide.

"Emily, is that really you?"

"Yes." Fingers began to protrude through the hole, wiggling down at her.

Kiami lifted herself onto her toes and brushed the tips of Emily's fingers with her own. "I can reach you, sort of."

"Stand back."

She backed up from the wall. "Are you..."

There was a dull thud above her, followed by a grunt. She thought she could hear Justin's faint voice and then another thud. Small pieces of debris trickled down to the floor, making plinking noises as they landed. Kiami took another large step back before Justin could hit the wall again.

A few rocks in the corner separated, and Kiami could hear them grinding against one another as Justin yelled out with the effort of his actions.

"Kiami?" Emily yelled down, her voice echoing against the walls. "Can you get through here in owl form?"

She stepped forward to look at the damaged wall. It looked as though they had managed to pull a few large chunks up through the opening on their side. The crack was now about two feet wide. "I could, but Emily?"

"What is it?"

"I think maybe it would be a better idea if you guys came in."

Several minutes of silence passed before Kiami called up again. "I can catch you, Emily, and you can help me catch Justin."

Emily dangled a foot through the hole. "Are you ready?"

"Sure." She watched as another foot slid through. She reached up and tapped one of the sneakers to prove she was in position.

More of Emily's legs began to appear as she wiggled her way

into the dungeon from above. Once Kiami could see her waist, she wrapped her arms around the protruding legs to help steady her descent.

Emily's head appeared, her arms still stretched upward. "Justin, you can let go."

Kiami held firmly to steady Emily as she finished dropping through the hole. She stumbled back a step as Emily's body bent forward in her arms.

She closed her eyes as she adjusted to the weight. When she was sure she had her balance back, she lowered Emily's feet to the floor.

Justin stood next to them. "You nearly gave her a heart attack." Emily reached out and cuffed Justin playfully on the arm.

Justin shrugged. "She can turn into an owl. Besides, I'm sure Amanda taught her a thing or two about us before she sent her off with Aden."

Kiami nodded. "I guess I just wasn't expecting it. Where is Aden?"

Justin folded his arms over his chest. "He told us to wait for him outside of the castle." He shot a glare at Emily.

She responded by putting her hand on her hip and rolling her eyes. "And I told you. If the wisps wanted us to follow, there was a reason."

"So what are you saying, then? That Aden isn't coming back?"

Justin balked at Kiami's questions. "Do you think Amanda did something to him?"

Kiami shook her head. "No. Amanda cares about him."

"Are you sure? She has killed someone in cold blood before. Aden told us."

Emily's face had turned red, and she stared at Justin in disbelief. "No, that is not what he said at all."

"How can we help Amanda without him? He was the one that knew the truth." Justin threw his arms up in the air. "If we find out that he's dead, I will kill her myself. I don't care what they asked us to do."

"THEY are your family, and the jinn in that town are the closest thing to a family I have had in a long time."

Kiami moved between the two of them. She couldn't believe the way Emily and Justin were acting. "Could you two please explain to me what you are arguing about?"

Emily pointed a finger at Justin. "You need to grow up. First, you are jealous of Aden, and now you are trying to what? Avenge him for something that probably didn't even happen. Aden has defended Amanda's character every step of the way."

"That's all the more reason not to trust her."

Justin's fists were clenched at his sides, and Kiami thought she saw the flicker of something in his eye as she placed one hand on each of their shoulders. "Both of you take a deep breath." She waited for them to inhale and exhale before continuing. "What exactly did the jinn from town say?"

Justin threw his hands up and backed away as Emily began explaining what Gemma had told them about the myth of the world and how they had been asked to help Amanda.

As she spoke, Kiami tried to piece the new information together with the things that Amanda had said to her. After Emily finished filling her in on the events of the secret underground room, she couldn't help but feel that they were missing something.

Emily and Justin were both watching her, waiting for her response, expecting her to take a side. "I sort of agree with you both. Minus the killing part. I don't know the jinn from town, but I do feel like I am in the right place, and there has to be a reason I am here." The pair remained silent, so she continued.

"After what you have told me, I know I was right to let her take me. If she had tried to get into the village, who knows what would have happened... Amanda has some kind of stone that amplifies her power, and she has managed to get better control of her magic by attaching it to a staff. I think that if something bad has happened to Aden, we should be wary. We should restrain her..."

Justin interrupted, "And how do you suppose we can manage that?"

"It will be tricky." Kiami spun in a circle. "We wait here, because she won't be expecting to find the two of you."

Justin cleared his throat. "I can vanish."

"No, jinn cannot hide from Amanda that way. She knows that I can control humans with my song. So that is what she will be anticipating. She doesn't know that I can transform."

"So, we are bait?" Emily whispered.

Kiami shot her an apologetic look. "More like a distraction. Once I am sure she is convinced it's only the two of you, I will change back, hopefully catching her off guard."

Amanda carried the candelabra down the stairs in a trance-like state, her shoes clicking against the stones.

Kiami was her only hope at gaining the trust of Emily and Justin.

If she couldn't convince her of what had happened to Aden, she didn't know what she would do.

She waved her new staff in front of the wall that blocked her path and took a deep breath as the rocks shifted and moved out of her way. If she had any hope of getting help from Kiami, she would need to tell her everything. She hesitated briefly before stepping down into the dungeon and looked up at the still glowing gem. She was beginning to believe that the stone affixed to the top of her staff was somehow very important.

Maybe together we can figure it out, she thought as she continued through the doorway.

Cool water seeped into her shoes as they met the floor, and Amanda raised the candelabra to look up to where the crack in the wall had been when she herself had been a prisoner here.

Distracted by her mission after she had gained her freedom, she had forgotten all about it, and now it was a gaping hole. Water was coming in steadily enough that a quarter inch covered the entirety of the floor.

Could Kiami have done this? Amanda could make out a form covered head to toe under the covers on the bed. The silhouette looked too short, and Amanda squinted, trying to adjust to the dim lighting. "Kiami, it's getting wet down here..."

She placed the candelabra down on the small table and reached out to shake her sleeping guest. The blanket shifted with her touch, unveiling black, springy curls, and Amanda stepped back in surprise as Emily bolted upright.

A strangled gasp escaped Amanda's lips as something big pushed against her, shoving her down onto the wet floor. The candles flickered suddenly as a second intruder appeared next to her.

Why didn't I check the room when I saw the hole? Amanda pushed herself up from the floor. "What have you done with Kiami?" she shouted as she turned to Justin, her fist still clenched around her weapon.

Fire danced in his hand; the candelabra lay tipped on its side, now extinguished. A sudden loud shriek came from the hole as something white hurtled through it.

Amanda pushed her hands forward and whispered as she aimed the staff at it; the black diamond seemed to regain its glow in an instant, and swirls of dark mist engulfed the object, bringing it to the ground at her feet.

Emily screamed and pushed past her as she sank down into the water beside the projectile. "Kiami!"

Amanda stared down at the strange owl. The beautiful bird lay with its wings outstretched against the floor, taking slow, labored breaths.

"Kiami?" Emily called again, and Amanda sank down to the floor as understanding settled in.

Emily leaned over her friend, the static filling her ears even as she turned her head and screamed in Justin's direction, "Look what you have done!"

She watched as Justin stumbled back. "Me? I didn't do that."

"You weren't supposed to attack. What did you think Kiami would … do?" The wave was pushing at her, begging her to let go.

"Come on, please change back, Kiami." The bird only blinked up at her. "Please." *She can't…*

Dammit, there is no other way. She placed her hand on the bird and allowed her power to rush outward over Kiami, healing her.

The castle groaned around them as Kiami returned to human form and Emily turned her face up toward Amanda.

"I, I'm not doing it," Amanda whispered.

A thunderous boom echoed from outside as the castle groaned again. Debris shifted and fell from the ceiling. "Kiami, can you walk?"

She sat forward and rubbed the back of her head. "I think so."

Emily helped steady her as she pulled herself up off the floor. The air seemed to hum around them in a familiar way.

Amanda still stared blankly at the place where Kiami had been dying on the floor only moments earlier. "I'm sorry. I didn't know…"

"Save it. We need to go see what's happening outside." Another loud boom echoed all around them as Emily held her free hand out toward Amanda to help her up. "Come on."

Instead of accepting her help, Amanda pushed herself up from the floor and turned to face Kiami, her eyes searching for a response. "I am sorry."

Emily wasn't sure how much her healing magic had actually helped Kiami. She seemed to need to use her as a crutch in order to maintain an upright position, and her own chest now felt tight. She was relieved when Kiami shifted some of her weight back to her own feet and finally nodded at Amanda.

33

Oh, Rats!

Amanda balked as Justin rushed ahead, the flame moving up his arm as he pushed past her.

He doesn't even know where he's going.

She signaled for the other two to move on ahead. Both Emily and Kiami walked as if they were in pain. Emily clasped Kiami's arm tightly; she seemed to cringe with each slow step, and Amanda couldn't help but wonder if Emily had taken on some of the damage inflicted on Kiami as her own.

Had she ever healed anyone so close to the brink of death before? Maybe her healing only went so far... Emily seemed to have remained kind and compassionate, despite the things she had endured. They were all so different. How was it possible that they were meant to work together?

Amanda steadied herself against the wall with one hand and firmly gripped her staff with the other as the castle groaned and shook again.

Justin had disappeared onto the main floor without a backward glance. As the castle stopped trembling, Emily looked down at Amanda, and she nodded. "Keep going."

When they rounded the corner, Amanda hung back and closed

her eyes. *Why are they even listening to me?*

Kiami tapped at Emily's shoulder when she stopped hearing the clinking noise of Amanda's shoes on the stone floor. She had the strongest urge to sing that she had ever remembered. *Was it brought on by the pain?* She leaned against the wall as Emily released her arm and headed down the winding stairs, disappearing from her sight.

I would have died if Emily wasn't there. How long has it been since I sang?

She had been unable to return to her human form after Amanda's attack, but even when Emily had healed her, she didn't feel fully restored. It seemed Emily's power could only fix so much. But still she had always been repaired when she had transformed before...

Was Jacqueline right all along? Have I been taking a tiny bit from everything around me, like a thief? Am I like a battery that needs to recharge? She ground her teeth, trying to hold her song in as Emily popped back around the corner with Amanda at her heels.

On the stairs and out of Kiami's sight, Emily had taken a moment to breathe. The pressure was intense, and her chest burned with the effort. She knew that the pain wouldn't go away until her body expelled whatever she took from Kiami.

She reached her hand into her pocket and squeezed the amethyst for courage.

The clinking of Amanda's shoes resumed as she came into her line of sight. Emily looked up into her eyes, expecting to see anger. Instead she only saw sadness and desperation.

They hadn't encountered Justin on their slow trip to the top floor, and Amanda hadn't felt the castle rumble in some time.

She led Emily and Kiami up to a narrow wall that ran along the outer edge of the castle's wall walk. The whole way up from the dungeon, she had felt wrong somehow, but she hadn't been able to place her finger on it until she stepped outside. It was too quiet, and the lack of water cascading down around the exterior of the castle was to blame.

The air felt heavy as she leaned against the parapet to see what was happening.

Flames lined Justin's shoulder blades where he stood on the ground below, and she clicked her tongue at his audacity and furrowed her brow.

What have I unleashed? Amanda wondered as she looked down on the spectacle.

A trio of girls stood in front of him in a semicircle, their hands interlocked. Curled hair hung in ringlets around their small, delicate faces. They wore identical frilly lace dresses that stopped at their knees and light blue sashes tied in big bows around their waists.

They looked sweet, and Justin seemed to be having an innocent conversation with them.

Amanda knew better than to believe it.

Their faces lifted to the sky as the three heads turned in unison toward her; even from this distance she could see that each girl had one large eye above their cute button noses.

Kiami watched as the flames along Justin's shoulder blades split in half and moved down his arms, filling the palms of his hands. Then he began waving his arms in the air, trying to draw the single-eyed girls' attention away from the castle.

They swiveled their heads around to him as one and then tilted them backward, opening their mouths wide. The pitch of their laughter carried up to her; the shrill, screeching noises sounded more animal than human to her sensitive ears.

She looked over to where Amanda watched, thumbing her nails against the battlement. *What is she waiting for? Why doesn't she do something?* Suddenly Amanda's eyes went wide, and Emily screamed in surprise from beside her.

Kiami turned back to see what was going on. The one-eyed girls continued to laugh as they watched two knee-high brown animals advance on Justin.

The creatures had seemed to appear out of nowhere. They stood upright on their hind legs, and long, rat-like snouts protruded from their hairy faces. He lifted one hand toward the beasts, and the orange flame in his palm changed rapidly from red to blue before he threw his hand outward, causing the flame to leap up, out of his hand, and onto one of the rat creature's backs.

Kiami heard the creature let out a hideous scream before it

threw itself onto the grass, rolling back and forth. Justin raised his other flame-filled hand into the air, ready to attack the second creature, just as Kiami's view became obstructed.

Emily screeched again as the single-eyed monster girls began to change and grow. She reached for her stone, pulling it from her pocket and clutching it firmly in her palm. She hoped Justin could handle the two beasts that the monster girls had conjured before they themselves had begun to transform.

They weren't girls anymore, but rather one girl with three heads, and it kept getting taller... "What is that?" She had never witnessed anything like this before, and it all seemed to be happening too fast for her to keep up.

The three-headed manifestation turned toward her, each blinking its eye rapidly. "We are URD. From the realm of chaos." They spoke at once as they became level with and then rose over the side of the wall.

Except for the eye coloring, each head looked identical, even after this metamorphosis seemed to be complete. On the right the eye glowed amber, on the left a bright orange, and in the center head, a putrid dark green that reminded her of rotted seaweed.

Emily chewed at her lip as URD seemed to consider her a

moment, staring at her, before shifting its eyes in Amanda's direction to address her.

Amber eye spoke first. "You killed our master."

The green-eyed head nodded. "We will kill you as he, Abaddon, wanted."

The orange-eyed head frowned. "But we are free, we don't have to."

The first head smiled. "But we can."

"So, we should," the second head agreed.

"They could still stop it," the third head said.

They continued to speak in turn, starting again from right to left.

"Can they?"

"They might."

"Yes."

"Unlikely."

"Impossible."

"Nothing is impossible."

Amanda stared at URD. *They are talking about Abaddon. This is my fault.* Her palms felt sweaty as she raised her staff up in front of them. If she had taken down URD's master, she had to be able to do the same to this ... thing.

"Go ahead."

"Yes, do it."

"You're just making it worse."

"You mean better."

"For us."

"Don't boast."

"We do what we can."

"We do what we have to."

"We are dying."

The first two heads turned inward toward each other, as if considering what the third head had said, before adjusting again to face Amanda. She lowered her staff back to the ground, unsure of how to proceed.

"Then we might as well kill one."

"So that they can't fix what they broke."

"That was the master's wish, not ours."

"Others have made it out since it started."

"Why can't we have any fun?"

Amanda became aware that Emily had moved beside her. She wouldn't have to fight alone. The weight of the magic between them seemed to fill the air. She raised her staff again, just as the third head answered.

"Do what you want." A smile spread across all three faces as Amanda began to whisper a spell, concentrating her shadow magic through the staff and onto URD.

Kiami had been weighing her options as she listened to URD's strange conversation.

She still didn't feel like herself; the urge to sing was beating at her, and she wanted to let go, but she would run the risk that her voice would affect Amanda and Emily. And it was entirely possible that it wouldn't affect URD at all.

I could transform and scratch URD's eyes out... Then she ran the risk of getting caught in Emily and Amanda's powers if they decided to attack.

How can I help?

Unsure of what would be more effective against the monster, Kiami began to feel useless. She was stuck.

A piercing scream was carried up to her sensitive ears. She had forgotten all about Justin. *My singing doesn't affect him.*

Divide and conquer. Without further hesitation, Kiami climbed up onto the ledge and willed herself to change. As soon as she felt the first prickle of magic raise the hair on her arms, she dove down head first.

As she watched the ground rush toward her, she thought she had made a terrible error in judgment. Then, suddenly, her wings spread, and she began to glide. She poised her claws for attack and swooped in to scratch at the menacing creatures' faces.

Kiami could bet from the sight that if she was still in human form, the smell of burned hair would have filled her nostrils. The beasts were covered in singed and bloody fur, they looked battered and beaten, yet they still would not stop going after Justin. She shifted her goal to him, intending to land behind him as she willed herself to change back.

This time her transformation was even slower. Minutes seemed to tick by before she was once again in full human form, and she couldn't help but wonder if she was still being affected by her recent trauma in the dungeon.

The air around her felt heavy as she breathed. Her normally excellent vision was distorted. Her surroundings seemed opaque and hazy, as if a light fog engulfed the land, and she squinted, trying to focus on the location of the rat creatures.

Just as she opened her mouth to sing, one of the rat creatures rushed at her, knocking her backward to the ground. The rat snarled, baring its sharp teeth, and lunged for her throat. There was a sudden rush of wind as its weight was lifted from her chest, and she watched as Justin began to wrestle with the creature on the ground.

She caught sight of the second rat creature a few yards away. It moved toward her at a steady pace as she jumped up to her feet, never taking her eyes from it. It slowed as a dark brown blur of movement circled it, and then a low growl rose from beside her and the rat creature began moving toward her again, now hobbling as it walked.

Fizzle? Shocked that the small animal would try to defend her in such a way, Kiami's eyes darted around the field, but she couldn't catch more than a brief blur of the fuzzy animal's movements as it taunted the rat creature by running in circles around it.

She heard Justin yell out behind her and spun in his direction.

He had lost his hold on the first rat creature again, and it was barreling in her direction at an alarming rate. Kiami planned stay put as long as possible and to sidestep out of its path, but when she looked down, Fizzle was at her feet, staring up at the approaching rat creature with his tiny black eyes.

Kiami let out a strangled noise as Fizzle's long, white tongue lashed out at her attacker, wrapping it around one of its legs and causing it to stumble forward face first onto the ground.

She stared in disbelief as Fizzle slurped his tongue back into his mouth and darted forward, disappearing into the hazy field. Kiami directed her attention back to the rat creature that Fizzle had taken down. She watched as it pushed itself back up to its feet, but it made no effort to continue its attack. It seemed to be in a daze.

Something hit her lightly on the shoulder, and she jerked around. It wasn't often that someone could sneak up on her, but she had been so focused on the rat creature that she hadn't registered Justin's approach.

"I knew there was something weird about that fuzz ball. Look at what the other one is doing." The second rat creature also appeared to be stunned; he would move forward a few feet and then stop to look around before turning and repeating the motions. "I think he's got something in his saliva."

Kiami raised her eyebrows. "What are you talking about? Fizzle?"

"The effects are temporary. It causes something like confusion or calmness..."

"Are you trying to say that Fizzle did that to me?"

"The point is it's temporary, and they could snap out of it at any moment unless we do something to keep them from retaliating."

"What about Amanda and Emily?" Kiami looked up toward

where the side of the castle should have been, but in the haze all she could make out was a large, swirling black mass that seemed to engulf everything, starting from the ground upward in that direction.

"They have got this."

She turned back to Justin. "Are you sure?"

"Is there another option?"

Kiami shook her head. She still didn't know if her music would affect the rat creatures, but right now it seemed her only usable defense. She opened her mouth and began to sing, low at first then higher. She had never been so drained before, and as the music flowed she closed her eyes, aware that if unaffected, the rat creatures could attack at any moment. If they did, she hoped that Justin would have her back.

Emily knew she couldn't hold on to the wave of magic much longer. Then her breath caught in her throat as she watched Kiami leap from the side of the castle while still in her human form. It was all she could do to stop the magic from pouring out of her at that moment.

She turned to Amanda as if in slow motion and watched her fist tighten around the staff as URD continued to debate whether or not to attack her.

Emily had only gotten a quick glimpse of Amanda's shadow magic before. When she used it on Kiami, there had been a quick flash, and it had been over. This was different, and she found herself temporarily transfixed by the sight as shadowy tendrils spewed out of the gemstone.

It wasn't until the steady static sound that had been beating at her eardrums intensified, muffling URD's voice so that she could barely make out the creature's final responses, that she remembered herself. The shadowy tendrils had already engulfed URD.

Too tired to fight it any longer, she gave in and allowed the wave that had been building up inside her since she had healed Kiami to burst from her. As the wave washed over URD, she saw Amanda lift her staff higher. The gem affixed at the top seemed to glow even brighter. URD threw its arms up as it stumbled backward, and the inky shadows shifted, revealing its still smiling faces.

The weight of the magic no longer affecting her, Emily rushed forward to the edge of the wall and peered down as URD landed on its back with a thud that reverberated through the ground, shaking the castle as it landed.

She watched as Kiami picked herself up from the grass and reached out to pull Justin to his feet.

URD's form began to flicker in and out of view. The air around her hummed once again as if electrified, and she turned to Amanda just as a blast of cold air hit her.

Amanda rubbed at her arms. The wind howled around her. White stuff swirled through the air. *Snow...* She had never seen snowfall in the Arcane realm.

She called out, "What is going on?" to anyone that could hear her.

"HERE."

Blinded by the storm, she took a step toward the sound of Emily's voice and reached forward. Her shoes sank down into the snowdrift, and cold prickled her exposed skin.

Just as she managed to grasp Emily, the humming that filled her ears stopped. The world in front of her appeared to waver and ripple in a way that reminded her of an undisturbed pond that suddenly had a large stone tossed into it. Before she could form a logical question to ask, the scene dissolved completely, and the piercing cold had been replaced by the mild temperature she was used to in the Arcane realm.

Amanda could once again feel solid stone beneath her shoes. Confused, she turned her head from side to side to take in her surroundings. They were back atop the castle. She let go of Emily and turned in a circle, looking for any sign of the snow.

Justin and Kiami stared back at her and Emily, slack-jawed, and as she pushed past the pair and into the castle, she heard

Kiami ask, "Where did you guys go?"

That's what I would like to know, she thought as she hurried down to the library, her hands still numb from the frigid temperature she had been exposed to.

34

Catching On

Kiami knew where Amanda was headed, and she turned on her heels to follow, motioning for Emily and Justin to join them.

By the time she led them all to the library, Amanda was already hunched over a book.

Justin tugged at her arm, whispering, "Kiami, what are you doing?" She turned to face him. Scratches ran the length of his arms. "Why are we following her? We can't just let her do what she wants. She still hasn't even told us where Aden is." As he spoke, blood oozed down his shirt from a small gash below his chin.

She took a deep breath; he looked awful. The rat creatures had done quite a number on him before Fizzle had intervened, allowing her time to enthrall them with her song.

When she started to sing, she had been drained, but the longer she let the music flow from her, the more she felt her energy return. What remained of her own injuries had healed up after she transformed to fly back up to the top of the castle.

She blushed and looked down at her feet. Even though she didn't have the ability to control a jinni, she had to wonder if she had taken something from him as well during the fight, given his haggard appearance.

He choked out his next words. "Kiami, I want to go home."
His face had turned a deep shade of crimson. Having grown up
knowing his heritage, she had thought that he would have had
the easiest time accepting everything that had happened, but the
opposite seemed to be true, and she wasn't sure how to help him.

Emily had never seen a library like this before, and her immediate reaction was to begin inspecting the stacks of books. She ran
her fingers along the spines, feeling the different textures of the
covers as she circled the dimly lit room, allowing them to glide
naturally over the smooth leather and abrasive cloth. Content,
she had made it three quarters of the way around the room when
she paused and lifted her fingers.

This book felt different. She inspected the wooden spine more
closely. *Someone hand-carved this.* Curious, she slowly pulled
the book from its resting place, giving the carved sapling and
runes on its cover only a moment's glance before she began
thumbing through the yellowed pages, but she couldn't make
out the strange language.

She was just about to snap the book closed when she noticed the
triangle corner of a paper that didn't match the rest sticking out

from the side. She flipped through to the folded note's resting place and opened it alongside the book's current page.

As she skimmed the contents, she could hear Kiami and Justin whispering. Emily tore her eyes from the confession and looked up at the pair. They both appeared to be quite upset.

She folded the page back in half. Now was not the time to show them the letter she had found. Still, she knew she should hold on to it. She flipped the wooden book closed and stuffed it under her arm as she instead approached Amanda.

"What do you think? Did you figure something out?"

"I have a theory. Did you hear URD say she was from the Chaos realm?"

Emily gave a nod. "It shouldn't be possible, should it?"

"No, but somehow, I think we were also pulled into a different realm." She held up a book to show Emily a drawing of a snow-covered land.

"That's where we went?"

"I can't be a hundred percent sure..." Amanda looked up into her eyes. "Do you hear that?"

Emily shook her head as she spoke. "I don't hear anything except the constant droning of that blasted waterfall."

"Exactly," Amanda croaked.

"What do you mean?"

"When URD showed up, the waterfall stopped flowing, and now it's back."

Emily took a step closer and spoke softly. "Amanda, if Aden is not coming, we need to return to the Human realm."

Amanda looked around wildly for a moment. "I should stay here."

Emily placed a hand on her shoulder and shook her head before answering, "Please come back with us."

"But the library."

"Take anything you think is useful. Maybe the jinn in town can help answer some of your questions."

Amanda gave a slow nod, and Emily squeezed her shoulder again. "Whatever is happening, you won't have to face it alone."

Justin had been listening and scoffed, "Really, Emily?"

She let go of Amanda and pivoted toward him. "If you can't do it for your family, then do it for me." *This has to stop.* She needed to address the real issue. She reached forward to grab hold of his hand. "I understand why you felt betrayed when you found out that Cherry and Gemma were keeping things from you. Maybe their behavior even made you question if you belong?"

Justin looked into her eyes before giving her hand a light squeeze. "How will we even manage to get back?"

Kiami spoke up. "Amanda will take us, won't you?"

Amanda nodded slowly, the words of URD's master, Abaddon, replaying in her head. *They will never trust you*

About the Author

M. Ainihi is a passionate YA Fantasy Author, proud Mother, Wife, and Adventurer. Hailing from the wilds of Upstate New York and currently residing in the Chicagoland area, Lost is the second novel in a planned quartet.

You can connect with me on:
- https://mainihi.wordpress.com/
- https://twitter.com/m_ainihi
- https://www.goodreads.com/author/show/17165495.M_Ainihi

Also by M. Ainihi

Rise: A Blood Inheritance Novel
Most humans do not know about the existence of the outer realms, or the fierce battles that once waged between the magical races before their creation. But for teen Amanda, ever since she encountered the jinni in the forest, it's her new reality, a place where darkness lies around every corner, and she's lost almost all hope of surviving it.

Endow: A Blood Inheritance Novel
Coming Soon...